Dear Reader

Welcome to Nikki and Fraser's story. These two have their share of issues to resolve, stemming from those uncertain teenage years when they, like the rest of us, were finding out about themselves and putting their toes in the dating waters.

I've set this story around the ambulance service as I have a lot of admiration for the people who regularly face situations that would have most of us hiding under a blanket. The exacting standards of care and service are a credit to each and every member of the New Zealand St John Ambulance Service.

I personally spent time working with the crews at Blenheim Station, but for the purposes of this book have used fictitious characters and events.

But in the end this story is about Nikki and Fraser finding their way back to each other. I hope you enjoy it.

Until next time...

Cheers!

Sue

PS I'd love to hear from you, so drop me a line on sue.mackay56@yahoo.com or visit my website at www.suemackay.co.nz

With a background of working in medical laboratories and a love of the romance genre, it is no surprise that **Sue MacKay** writes Mills & Boon® Medical Romance™ stories. An avid reader all her life, she wrote her first story at age eight—about a prince, of course. She lives with her own hero in the beautiful Marlborough Sounds, at the top of New Zealand's South Island, where she indulges her passions for the outdoors, the sea and cycling.

CHRISTMAS WITH DR DELICIOUS

BY
SUE MACKAY

MILLS & BOON®

All the characters in this book have no existence outside the imagination of the author, and have no relation whatsoever to anyone bearing the same name or names. They are not even distantly inspired by any individual known or unknown to the author, and all the incidents are pure invention.

First published in Great Britain 2012
by Mills & Boon, an imprint of Harlequin (UK) Limited.
Large Print edition 2013
Harlequin (UK) Limited, Eton House,
18-24 Paradise Road, Richmond, Surrey TW9 1SR

ISBN: 978 0 263 23111 3

Harlequin (UK) policy is to use papers that are natural, renewable and recyclable products and made from wood grown in sustainable forests. The logging and manufacturing process conform to the legal environmental regulations of the country of origin.

Printed and bound in Great Britain
by CPI Antony Rowe, Chippenham, Wiltshire

Also by Sue MacKay:

EVERY BOY'S DREAM DAD
THE DANGERS OF DATING YOUR BOSS
SURGEON IN A WEDDING DRESS
RETURN OF THE MAVERICK
PLAYBOY DOCTOR TO DOTING DAD
THEIR MARRIAGE MIRACLE

These books are also available in eBook format from www.millsandboon.co.uk

This book is dedicated to all my extended family.
You've always been there for me
through all those blips life tosses up.
Love you all.

And to the Cancer Society of New Zealand,
especially the Blenheim and
Christchurch branches. You are awesome.
Thank you so much for your care and concern.

CHAPTER ONE

'OKAY, everyone, listen up.' Mike, the Blenheim Ambulance Base manager, strode purposefully into the staffroom and straddled a chair. 'I've just been talking to the boffins in Nelson.'

Nikki lifted her head from her laptop where she had been engrossed in her studies. Any conversation between Nelson, where their overall boss worked from, and Blenheim stations usually had a direct effect on everyone. 'What now?' she asked with a grin. 'Got to cut back on our coffee intake?'

Mike grinned back as he shook his head. 'Nothing so drastic. We've employed a paramedic, starting in eight days' time.'

Good news for once. 'That's going to lighten the workload for some of us.' They had plenty of volunteers working as ambulance officers but few full-time paramedics and advanced paramedics, which meant she was always being called in to work extra shifts. Not that she minded most of the time. More shifts meant more pay to spend at the fashion shops.

Mike hadn't finished. 'Gavin, I intend putting the two of you together so you can mentor him as he trains for his Advanced Paramedic qualification. I think you'll get on well with him. He comes across as confident and competent, as well as likeable.'

Gavin's face turned thoughtful. 'Why not Nikki? She's just as capable as me.'

Unused to Gavin questioning anything, Mike looked taken aback. 'She is, but at the moment this is how I want it to run. Okay?'

'Sure.' But Gavin looked worried.

To give him a break Nikki asked, 'So who is this person? Anyone we know?'

'I doubt it. He's been in Dunedin for years, but has decided to move back home. His credentials were too good not to take him on immediately. He could get a job anywhere in New Zealand if he wanted.'

Nikki shivered. A guy returning home from Dunedin after years away. Why should that raise her antenna so quickly? Quite a few people from here had gone to university in Dunedin and not come back. She glanced up at Mike but saw nothing more than enthusiasm for his new staff member. Another shiver tripped through her. 'Do we get a name for this guy?'

Mike's gaze remained fixed on her. 'Fraser McCall.'

The air left her lungs in a whoosh. The warning shaking her body had been right. 'That doesn't make sense. Are you talking about Fraser Ian McCall? Twenty-seven years old?'

'The same man.' Mike frowned. 'Problem?'

Yes. A big one. Panic squeezed her, turned her skin icy. Fraser could not work here, in this station, with her. He could not. It was too small. They'd always be running into each other, even if they were on opposing shifts. Did he know she worked here? If he did then it was unfair of him to even contemplate joining up. Why had he? 'He's a doctor, not a paramedic.'

Mike stood up. 'Wrong. McCall's been working on the ambulances for three years.'

Really? Why? Five years ago Fraser had just finished his fourth year at med school so that left two years between then and now unaccounted for. Of course, she hadn't heard anything about him since she'd returned home from Dunedin but he must've finished his studies at university in that time. Swallowing hard to push away the sudden blockage in her throat, she croaked, 'What was he doing before he joined the ambulance service?'

'You know I can't give out confidential information about any of the staff, including you, Nikki.' There was a warning, a message, in Mike's eyes just for her.

Hadn't Fraser mentioned to Mike he knew her? That they had history not easily dismissed? Hell, that they couldn't possibly work together? For five long years Fraser had shown he didn't give a damn about what had become of her. Why would he start now?

'Does he know I work here?'

'Yes. He seemed surprised. Said he knew you when you were a chef, and that you hadn't had a medical thought in your head.'

She dipped her head in acknowledgement. 'True.' Unexpected pain lashed at her. Was that all he admitted to remembering about her? What about the part where he had been her fiancé? Or that they'd lived together for three years? Been high-school sweethearts?

Her brain ran into overdrive, trying to assimilate the one piece of news she'd never, ever expected to be told. Or wanted to hear. Her hands clenched in her trouser pockets. How could she work with the man who'd once sworn he loved her so much he'd broken his own vow and proposed before he'd finished his training?

The man who had not shown up for their wedding, leaving her looking a complete fool, shaking in her high heels and beautiful silk gown, clinging to her father's arm as they'd stood on the top step ready to walk the aisle. To her love, her bright and exciting future.

They'd waited, and waited, she and her dad. Slowly her mother had joined them, then her four brothers had surrounded them, protecting her from the buzz of questions rising from the guests also waiting.

At the time she'd been frantic, thinking the worst, imagining him in a hospital bed after an accident, but he hadn't been there. Or anywhere she'd called. It had been as though he'd vanished into thin air. Then late that night he'd called her from who knew where. It had been the call she'd have given anything not to receive.

'Nik, I'm so sorry. About today, about everything. I won't be marrying you. Not ever. I'm sorry.' Fraser had choked and then the line had gone dead. As far as she knew, he hadn't been seen in Blenheim since.

The pen in Nikki's fingers shook, creating wonky lines as she filled in the weekly checklist for Blenheim One ambulance. Her teeth pressed into her top lip, inflicting a sharp pain. 'What's wrong with me this morning?' She couldn't blame the icy chill from the late winter frost blanketing Blenheim.

Fraser McCall. That's what's wrong.

'I know.' Her teeth dug harder.

So what are you going to say to him first? Hi, and welcome. Or, where've you been hiding for the past five years since you ran out on me?

'Definitely not that. That'd be telling him how much I still care and that's a non-starter.'

Since hearing from Mike that her worst nightmare was coming true she'd lived in dread of this day. Her stomach had been rioting continuously, barely tolerating even the tastiest food. The belt on her trousers was a notch tighter. Her mind had refused to shut down at night, giving a constant recital of all the reasons why she did not want to work with Fraser.

There'd been little sleep, causing her head to ache continuously. The headache pills she'd swallowed an hour ago hadn't worked, as they hadn't for the past eight days. And now her hands had started this crazy shaking that made her writing look like a two-year-old's.

How challenging could working with Fraser be? How difficult was it to run a marathon over mountains with no preparation? Her hands shook harder. Mike had put them on the same four-day roster, and no amount of pleading had changed that. She'd even baked Mike's favourite coffee and walnut cake, but had got zip, *nada*, nothing. At least she'd be working days while Fraser did the nights, and vice versa. Hopefully they'd only see each other at shift changeover. Still, far too often.

Toughen up. Use the opportunity to finally ask him why he left. Why he couldn't face marrying you. Why he didn't have the gumption to face up to you that day and tell you straight. Then you can tell him exactly how much you hurt at the time and that you're now totally over him.

'I am?' Of course she was. 'I'm older and wiser. I've learned not to trust as easily—which has to be a good thing, right?' Whatever. But she did have her future all mapped out, which went to show how far she'd moved on from Fraser.

A lonely future without a husband or children of your own.

'There's a wee niece or nephew due in six months' time. How cool's that?'

Not the same as your own. True. One day she'd love to have a baby, to feel it grow inside her, to push it out into the world and then smother it in love.

'Talking to yourself again?' Mike asked from the internal garage door.

'Only way to get a sensible answer,' she quipped automatically, while bending down to check the tread on the rear tyres. She didn't want Mike to see the pain and worry that must surely be swimming in her eyes.

'You're early. There's fifteen minutes until you clock on at seven.'

'I was up and ready so decided I might as well come in.' She'd figured it would be better to already be working when Fraser arrived. That way she could acknowledge his presence and then immediately carry on with the job. She straightened up slowly, made a show of ticking another box.

'Like you do that often.' When she glanced across the garage, Mike's calm, knowing smile beamed at her. 'Our newest crew member's also early.'

'What?' Fraser was here already? Shouldn't she have sensed his presence? Breathe in deeply, breathe out. In, out. It was too soon to front up to him. She wasn't ready. She'd never be ready. The next tick on the checklist skewed sideways. 'Dang.' She could do without this ridiculous thumping in her chest and the sudden lump blocking her throat. What did she say to him? It wasn't as though they could ever become friends again. Could they? No, too much pain sat between them.

'Nikki, you'll be fine. Whatever your problem is with Fraser, you're a very professional AP and I know you won't let anything come between you and your job.' Mike's words soothed her a little. If he believed she could manage then she'd do her best to live up to his expectations.

'I wish I was as confident as you.' She'd even mentioned resigning to Mike a couple of days ago but he'd known it for the halfhearted gesture it had been. She loved working as an AP and this was the only full-time ambulance station within a hundred kilometres. Her plans for owning a catering business were for the future, not now when she could help so many people when they were ill or distressed.

Mike stepped closer, the concern in his eyes worrying. 'Fraser's in the tearoom. Come and have a coffee, break the ice while everyone's around. You have to get past this moment, whatever's causing it.'

Gulp. There was another option. She could run away. *So you're a coward now? Face it, Fraser can't hurt you any more. That's done and dusted. And he was the one who did the running away, remember?* Pushing her shoulders back, sucking in another deep breath, she plonked the checklist down on the front seat of the ambulance and squeaked, 'You're right.' She owed this man who'd given her a break and taken her on at a time when he'd had many applicants, some far more qualified than her. Tapping his shoulder, she gave a weak smile. 'Thanks.'

At the tearoom door her shaky resolution backed off. Standing with his back to her, talking to Chloe and Ryan, who were about to take over on Blenheim Two for the day shift, was Fraser. Her first glimpse of him since she'd come home from Dunedin to get ready for their wedding, fully expecting him to follow her three weeks later.

Her heart bumped hard against her ribs as she drank in the sight of him. Fraser's tall, lean body had morphed into a broader, more muscular version of the body she'd known intimately. On Fraser the very ordinary uniform looked like something out of a style magazine. The black pants hugged his mouth-watering butt in a way that made her fingers itch.

What had seemed difficult had just become darned near impossible. Right now her heart was squeezing tight with raw longing, and her eyes were filling as an alien tenderness overtook her. Transfixed, she drank in the sight of this man who'd dominated her thoughts one way or another for all her adult life.

She swallowed, hard. 'Hello, Fraser.'

He turned slowly. Nervous? Unwilling to face her? It had never occurred to her over the past few days that he might find this situation as difficult as she was. But maybe he did. After all, he still owed her an explanation, not to mention an apology.

'Nikki.' He gulped. 'You're looking good.' His rich, golden-honey voice washed over her, bringing with it a storm of sweet memories.

Memories that until this moment she'd believed she'd deleted from her mind. Fraser murmuring to her as they'd lain tangled in the sheets of their small double bed in the cosy flat they'd shared with two other med students in Dunedin. Fraser egging her on to beat him at strip poker then laughing like crazy when she'd lost.

Stop it. Focus. Concentrate. Remember everything else. The burning humiliation, the pain in her heart so big she thought she'd die.

Nikki stared at him, speech impossible. He looked...different. That full, generous mouth, strong jaw line, the autumn-brown eyes all were tight with wariness instead of the constant laughter she remembered. But that was the least of the changes. His face had deep lines running either side of his mouth. A jolt of shock ripped through her as she looked further. His once straight, thick, chocolate-brown hair was streaked with grey, and curls spun over the tops of his ears, coiled at the edge of his collar.

What had happened? Was that why he'd done a runner? No. She refused to accept that as an excuse for his actions. If anything had gone wrong he'd have told her, and they'd have sorted it—together.

From somewhere a long way away Mike said, 'Let's have coffee while it's quiet. Fraser, you'll be pleased to know Nikki puts her cooking skills to great use and keeps us supplied with yummy treats.'

Nikki jumped. For a brief moment she'd forgotten where she was. A quick look around the staffroom showed Gavin and Amber watching this meeting with interest, as were the other day crew, who'd just arrived. Amber, her friend and flatmate, should've clocked off by now, but had probably hung around to meet the new guy.

Questions blazed from her eyes, warning Nikki there'd be an interrogation later.

Fraser spoke into the silence. 'My stomach's doing flips already.'

Nikki looked into his eyes, really looked, and locked gazes with him. She saw pain and resignation, determination and wariness, all tumbled together. None of the extreme confidence she'd known before. Again, shock tilted her sideways.

'So, how are you?' he asked softly.

Her chin pushed forward. 'Fine, good, busy.' *Dumbstruck, clueless about how to deal with you.*

'It is really good to see you. You look different somehow.' Fraser's tone sounded genuine, as his eyes appraised her slowly.

Too darned slowly. Making her skin heat. Drying her mouth. Huh? What was going on here? Had to be the sleepless nights catching up with her. Why else would she be feeling these odd sensations for a man she no longer trusted enough to make her a coffee?

Fraser moved forward, his arms lifting in her direction. To hug her?

Yikes. No way. Not now, not here. Not ever.

Quickly shoving her right hand out, she gripped his, shook it perfunctorily and let go. But not before something she hadn't felt for five years zinged up her arm. Desire.

Fraser heard Nikki mutter, 'Dang.' She spun away, her thick dark blonde plait swinging across her back as she added, 'I need coffee.'

Fraser grimaced. He could relate to that. Strong, black coffee might just fix what ailed him. Temporarily.

As if the mess he'd created way back when he'd learned he wasn't invulnerable could ever be fixed. Even with the best reasons in the world there was no denying he'd mucked up big time. Especially with this woman standing within reaching distance and looking as remote as the top of the Himalayas.

He couldn't prevent himself watching every movement Nikki made as she crossed to the whiteboard where case studies were written up for everyone to read and learn from. Despite the bulky green jacket she wore she seemed leaner than he remembered. Her steps were more deliberate, as though she'd lost the constant spring in her walk. Nikki Page. The girl he'd cherished at school. The woman he'd desperately wanted to marry. The lady he'd walked away from. Walked? Sped from, more like. He'd broken her heart. He'd also broken his own. Completely.

But he'd eventually got over her. Or so he'd thought. He'd truly believed that or he'd never have come to work here, despite how much he needed to become an AP for his father's sake.

'How do you take your coffee, Fraser?' Mike waved a mug at him, thankfully shifting his focus for a second.

'Black, thanks.' His gaze instantly returned to Nikki. Hell, a few moments ago he'd nearly hugged her. Why? Trying to prove that seeing her again was easy, that he had no hang-ups from the past? Proving it to Nikki? Or himself? Suddenly he felt unsure of everything—his plans to remain in Blenheim and settle down, his yearning to claw back the friendships he'd known before he'd messed up.

'I've got some cereal here for our breakfast,' the girl introduced to him as Amber told Nikki. Then waved the box at him. 'Fraser?'

Nikki's shoulders rolled. 'Not hungry at the moment.'

'Me neither.' He'd forced some toast down before leaving home twenty minutes ago, nearly gagging as it had stuck in his throat. Tiredness dragged at his body after he'd spent half the night pacing the house, keeping away from his parents' room in case he woke his light-sleeping mother. He'd asked himself repeatedly if coming to work here was the right thing to do, and had repeatedly come up with the same answer. It wasn't, and yet it was if he was getting on with his new life.

Amber shook the cereal box. 'You've got to have some food, Nikki. You've hardly eaten anything for days now.'

Nikki winced. 'Okay, just a little to appease you, bossy.'

So Nikki's appetite had disappeared lately. Since she'd heard he was coming to work at the same station? Strange, but he couldn't possibly affect her any more, could he? Not after the damage he'd done before. The way he'd treated her had been truly bad, despite his justifiable reasons.

'I'm bossy?' Amber chuckled. 'That's rich.'

'That's what friends are for. Keeping you in line.' Nikki shrugged eloquently and rubbed out a word on the board, rewrote it spelled correctly. 'Gavin, your spelling is atrocious. And don't go blaming your Welsh background. We might speak funny in New Zealand but the words are the same.'

Gavin looked up from the paper and spoke in what sounded like a put-on broad Welsh accent. 'You're right, Amber. She's nothing if not officious.' His wink showed how unfazed he was by Nikki's comments. 'So, Fraser, what brings you back to Blenheim? If you don't mind me asking, that is?'

'Family.' And getting on with the life he'd believed for so long he'd never get the chance to live. A second chance. 'My dad's not well so I want to be around to help out with things like keeping the house and section in order, making sure my mother's coping okay.'

Nikki's hand stilled on the board. Listening carefully? She asked without turning around, 'What's wrong with Ken?'

'He's got dementia.'

Nikki gasped, turned to look at him, sympathy in those wide azure eyes. 'That's terrible. Hard for your mum too, I imagine. I'm sorry, I didn't know.'

None of Nikki's family had had anything to do with his parents since that dreadful day when he'd hurt not just Nikki but two families who'd cared about him. He'd lost a lot of people who'd been important to him that day, but he only had himself to blame.

'Mum's managing but I think she's reaching her limits now that Dad's getting very argumentative and wanders a bit. That's why I've decided to live at home and not get my own place yet.'

Nikki nodded. 'I can hear your mum now, checking what time you get home at night, making sure you put your washing out. She'll be enjoying having you to watch over.'

There was a lot Nikki didn't know but she'd got that spot on. His mum had been devastated that he hadn't come home when he'd been diagnosed, but she certainly seemed intent on making up for that now.

Gavin leaned back in his chair. 'You can't beat

having your family around. They take precedence over everything else.'

There's no wedding ring on Nikki's finger. The thought blazed through him. *She's still single.* Hang on. No ring meant nothing. She could be in a relationship. Why not? A stunning-looking woman whom everyone adored would attract any red-blooded male. He should feel happy for her, not empty and sad. And maybe a tiny bit hopeful.

'Are your parents still living in Redwood Street?' Nikki stared at him. 'Fraser?'

He shook away those bewildering thoughts. 'Same old house that I grew up in. It's looking a bit tired now.' His mum was struggling with the maintenance. He should've come home sooner but no one had told him he was needed. Not until the night last month when he'd phoned his parents to give them the good news that his five-year tests had shown no sign of the cancer returning. The specialist had virtually given him an all-clear and a new lease on life.

His good news had been tempered with the information that his father had dementia and had had it for two years. It hurt that his mother had decided not to mention it while the cancer cloud had hung over him. Another black mark against him.

There'd been no time yesterday to track Nikki down and make contact prior to starting here. Neither had he found out anything about her, so he asked now, 'Are you living on the farm? Or in town somewhere?'

'Amber and I share a poky flat not far from here.'

No address, then. But what had he expected? An invitation to dinner? 'Most of town isn't far from here.'

Mike coughed. 'Can I see you two in my office? Now?'

Nikki's azure eyes blinked. 'Shouldn't Gavin be joining you? He's the one going to work with Fraser.'

Mike answered brusquely, 'No. Bring your coffee with you.'

At the table Gavin appeared totally absorbed in the newspaper.

What was up? Suddenly Fraser sensed he was about to learn something he definitely would not like. He knew that feeling. It started deep in his belly and writhed outwards, upwards, cold and insidious, taking over his body and then his mind. He'd known it once before and that time the news had been grim. He wanted to call out to Mike, to stop him before any words were uttered, but Mike had disappeared into his office.

At the door Nikki turned back to him, a huge question in her eyes. So she was worried too. He wished he had it in his power to take away that dread blinking back at him. Hell, she was still gut-wrenchingly beautiful. His heart slowed, his throat filled as he headed in the direction of the office they'd been summoned to. She still turned his head, still made him want to hold her and run his hands over her satin skin. Talk about bad timing for remembering those particular sensations. Nikki Page was a no-go zone.

Closing the office door was a mistake. He'd shut the three of them into the small space and there was no getting away from Nikki. He drew a deep, steadying breath. And inhaled her scent. The one that had always reminded him of summer gardens; of roses and freesias and peonies. For a brief moment his head spun, almost taking his feet out from under him. Placing a hand on top of the filing cabinet, he waited for his heart rate to slow to normal. And tried to concentrate on the dull, grey carpet under his black workboots.

Then Mike began to speak and he forgot everything as the dread he'd felt minutes ago became reality.

'Gavin handed me his notice last night. Patricia has been homesick for a while now so they're heading back to Wales next month.' Mike sat on the edge of his desk, his feet stretched between them. 'Nikki, you're taking his place as Fraser's mentor.'

'C-can't Gavin do it until he leaves? A month's a long time.' Her bottom teeth bit into her top lip and her wide eyes gleamed desperately at her boss. 'I can take over in September.'

'No, Fraser deserves continuity while he's training.' Mike hesitated, looked from Nikki to him and back to Nikki. 'Look, you two have obviously got history but if you're working here then you leave it at the door. Our patients deserve one hundred per cent concentration from all of us, all the time. I can't have you warring on the job.'

'That won't happen,' Fraser rushed to assure him.

Nikki's head snapped up and the glare that pierced him told him he shouldn't be so sure of that. But she did say, 'As long as we keep everything on a professional basis, it should work.' A breath escaped between her lips. 'I guess,' she added softly, the glare softening as worry and uncertainty took over.

Mike continued to outline what was expected of them both, then handed Fraser a folder, a key and a pager. 'Your rosters, course notes and timetable, and access codes.' He then shoved out his hand and clasped Fraser's. 'Again, welcome aboard. It's great to have someone experienced joining us. Isn't it, Nikki?'

Shaking Mike's hand, Fraser watched Nikki as she hauled herself off the chair. 'Yes, a change from training someone right from scratch.' Her voice was a monotone, as though she'd put a tight rein on herself. Was she barely keeping from yelling at him to go away, get lost?

Ah, Nik, if only you knew how much I regret

having done that to you once already. On everyone's belts pagers beeped simultaneously. Relief poured across Nikki's face as she snatched at hers. 'Priority one. We're on, Fraser.' And she was gone, charging out the door and into the garage before he'd taken a step.

He followed quickly, equally glad of the interruption while they both assimilated the new situation. But, damn, working in the same truck with Nikki would make everything a hundred times more difficult. They weren't being given any time to get used to being around one another. No time at all. Straight into the fire. Might be the best way.

CHAPTER TWO

NIKKI raced for the ambulance, leaving Fraser to follow. He might be used to a different station but the drill would be the same. Snapping her seat belt in place, she turned the ignition key as he slid into the passenger seat. 'Did you unplug the truck?' she asked, without looking at him.

'Yes. Having you drive off with the power supply still attached wouldn't be a good look on my first day.'

'It's been done before.' Mainly by new recruits eager to leap aboard, on their way to a call, and completely forgetting about all the truck's many batteries being kept topped up while on standby. With so much equipment on board that needed power, the batteries drained very quickly.

Fraser tapped the computer screen, bringing up the details of the callout. 'Ashleigh Rest Home. Eighty-seven-year-old woman found lying on bedroom floor. Conscious but groggy.'

'And probably very cold because of this morning's frost.' Putting on the lights and siren, she eased the ambulance out of the garage, nodding thanks to the car drivers giving way to them. If she concentrated on the details of the job and the traffic she was weaving the heavy vehicle through she might be able to pretend that wasn't Fraser sitting on the other side of the truck.

Who was she kidding? It was Fraser. No getting away from that. His size dominated the cab. The tantalising citrus smell of his aftershave teased her senses. He hadn't used aftershave before, not that she could remember, and she remembered most things about him. He liked scrambled eggs soft and made with cream, his toast underdone, his steak rare, and would refuse point blank to eat lumpy mashed potatoes.

Fraser fumbled around behind her seat. 'Where's the PRF kept?'

'Under your seat.'

He found the patient report form and copied in details from the screen, appearing totally impervious to the situation.

Why couldn't she act as though he was any

other crew member she had to mentor? She tried. 'Patient's name?'

'Mavis Everest.'

'Don't know her.' In a town the size of Blenheim she often attended people she knew, which added a personal, and not always welcome, factor to the situation. 'Is Mavis in a unit or the hospital wing?'

'A detached unit, number three. She must be capable of looking out for herself, then. Not bad at that age.'

'Probably has a caregiver.' Nikki hated the idea of anyone she loved ending up in a retirement village. A lot of people liked the security and companionship but she couldn't see her parents there after spending their lives on the farm. Not that they were even close to having to think about that but, still, she already knew she'd look after them if the need arose.

'Is this a good rest home?' Fraser asked, peering through the windscreen as the entrance came into view.

'I've never heard any complaints or noticed anything untoward. Why? Looking for somewhere to live?' Dang, why crack a joke? She was supposed to be keeping aloof and discussing work only.

Fraser's smile flicked on and off so fast she nearly missed it. 'No, thinking about my dad.'

'He's too young for this place.' She recalled Ken McCall as being years younger than her father. 'But I guess dementia doesn't take note of age.'

'Isn't that a fact? He's decades too young. But soon Mum has to face reality and put him into care. He's already a handful for her.' A haunting sadness filtered through Fraser's voice and into the cab between them.

'But she loves him. It can't be easy, making that decision.'

'No, it can't,' he snapped.

Whoa, what had she said wrong?

Then he said in a milder tone, 'Sorry. I'm still trying to get my head around it all.'

Nikki negotiated the narrow entranceway, her mind focused almost entirely on Fraser. His sadness made her want to do the strangest of things. Made her yearn to put her arms around him and hug him tight; made her wish his worries away.

Stop it. Let Fraser in at all and you're back

where he left off with you. It was a long enough haul getting over him the first time. Just remember the black hole of depression you fell into and that'll keep you well away from him.

With a hitch in her throat she drove into the parking area. How could she even be contemplating touching him or wanting to help him? That's what partners, husbands and wives, lovers did. Not estranged couples.

Finding unit three, Nikki prepared to back up to the tiny pathway leading to Mavis Everest's front door, checking as she went how low a nearby tree hung. Wiping off the emergency lights with a branch never went down well back at the station. A car was parked close to where she wanted to put the truck. She sighed. 'Why couldn't the staff have asked the car owner to shift?'

'Want me to direct you?' Fraser's hand was on the doorhandle.

'I've got it.' She backed up neatly and stopped. Jumping down, she headed for the back of the truck and pulled the doors open, tugged out the stretcher in readiness for their patient.

When Fraser picked up the defibrillator and

the pack containing their equipment, she nodded silently. He knew what he was doing.

A tall, gaunt woman in her late fifties opened the front door. 'Judy Mathers.' She sighed exasperatedly. 'I came around when Mum didn't answer her phone. We talk every morning at seven while I'm getting ready for work. I found her on the floor and I can't lift her back into bed.'

They squeezed into the stifling, tiny bedroom full of large furniture. At least their patient hadn't got hypothermic but how she'd found a space to fall was beyond Nikki. 'Mrs Everest, I'm Nikki and this is Fraser. How long have you been lying down there?'

'Been here all night.' Mavis Everest's voice was weak but there was a twinkle of mischief in her faded eyes. 'Long time since I spent the night on the floor alone.'

Unzipping her jacket, Nikki squeezed down beside the prostrate woman and smiled as she reached for Mavis's wrist. She hated seeing elderly people in this sort of predicament. It seemed so undignified and lonely somehow. 'Can you remember what happened?'

'Got up to go to the bathroom and felt a bit

dizzy. Must have blacked out because that's all I remember. Woke up some time about two.' When Nikki raised an eyebrow, Mavis added, 'The radio was on. The talkback show and some silly man complaining about his ingrown toenails and how the doctor wouldn't fix them.'

Mavis was alert and her speech coherent. All good indicators. Amazing, considering how long she'd been lying there. Nikki counted the steady beats under her fingertip as her watch ticked over a minute. Sixty-three. 'Normal,' she assured Mavis.

Fraser took Mavis's other hand. 'I'm going to check your blood-sugar level so just a wee prick in your finger, Mrs Everest.'

'Ooh, dear, don't go to any fuss. Just help me back into bed and I'll be good as gold.'

From the doorway Judy said in her exasperated tone, 'Do what they say, Mum, for goodness' sake. They know best. The sooner they've done with you, the sooner I can get off to work.'

Blimey, show some concern for your mother, why don't you? Nikki kept her face straight with difficulty.

Fraser deftly took a small sample of blood

from the elderly woman's thumb, speaking softly as he did so. 'We need to find out why you were dizzy, Mavis. Nikki's checking all your bones in case you did some damage when you fell.'

Nikki ran her hands over their patient's head, down her neck, feeling for contusions or abnormalities. Down Mavis's arms, torso and on down her legs. 'Looking good.'

'For an old duck,' Mavis quipped.

'You're only as old as you feel.' Fraser shoved the glucometer back in its bag. 'Glucose is four point six. No problems on that front.'

But a few minutes later he told Nikki, 'Blood pressure's low.'

Nikki nodded. 'That could explain how she ended up on the floor.' Looking up at Judy, she asked, 'Has Mrs Everest got a history of low blood pressure?'

'Doesn't look like it.' The woman held four pill bottles in her hand. 'Only arthritis drugs here.'

She doesn't know? 'Can you pop them in a bag for us? And some overnight clothes.' Nikki turned back to Mrs Everest. 'Mavis, have you ever had any problems with your blood pressure before?'

'Not that I'm aware of.'

'Okay. The doctor will do some more tests. We're going to take you to hospital now.'

'No, love, I don't want any fuss. My GP can visit when she's got time later today.'

'For pity's sake, Mum, just do as they tell you. If you weren't so stubborn about going into the partial-care wing of this place, we wouldn't be here now.'

Nikki felt her blood beginning to simmer but bit down on the retort itching to escape. This had absolutely nothing to do with her. 'Your GP would probably send you to hospital anyway, Mavis.'

'My daughter will be happy with that. Save her having to check up on me.' The yearning in the old lady's voice saddened Nikki.

'I'm sure she'll find time to visit you.' Or was that unrealistic? Nikki mightn't know anything about Judy or her own family commitments but she couldn't understand people who neglected their parents. Look at Fraser. His parents' woes had brought him home when nothing else had.

Fraser straightened up. 'I'll bring the stretcher inside. Mavis, you're going for the trip of your lifetime. First-class bed in the ambulance.' He winked down at the little lady in her winceyette nightgown.

'Do you serve meals as well?' Mavis rallied, a tired smile lifting her mouth.

'This is the drinks run. Saline via drip.'

Nikki gave Fraser a reluctant smile. This was the man she used to know. The man who'd always made people laugh with his light-hearted banter. 'Keep it up. You're making her feel better. I'll get the stretcher.' Laughter was definitely the best medicine. 'We need to get Mavis into her dressing gown to keep her warm outside. I'll also brush her hair to spruce her up a bit.' Warmth and dignity would be equally important to the elderly lady.

'Thanks, love. Can't go out looking like something the cat dragged in.'

Fraser picked up the thick robe and began to gently slip a sleeve up Mavis's arm. 'You're going to wow those doctors in ED by the time I've finished with you.'

Nikki strode outside for the stretcher and gasped. She'd been smiling. At Fraser, and how he handled Mavis so well. For a very brief moment she'd forgotten the past. Dang.

Thirty minutes later their patient had been delivered into the kind care of the ED nurses and Nikki pulled away from Wairau Hospital's ambulance bay. 'You were good with Mavis.'

Fraser picked up the handset. 'Why do you sound surprised?'

Gulp. Yeah, why did she? 'I'm not, really. You were always brilliant with patients.' She'd observed it first hand when he'd been training and she'd dropped by the hospital to see him. Changing the subject away from anything close and personal, she said quickly, 'Some old folk are so lonely. I wonder how they get that way. Mavis's daughter doesn't exactly seem overly caring and loving.'

'Maybe they've had a bust-up in the past. Life doesn't always pan out how you expect it to.' Fraser pressed the button and spoke to the call centre in Christchurch where all 111 calls in the South Island were dealt with.

Was she talking about his father? Or their relationship? Her life had certainly gone off course because of Fraser. But his voice had been harsh with knowledge, with deep understanding of things going wrong. Had he faced something terrible since before he'd left her? Or had it been the prospect of getting married that had distressed him so much? Not for the first time she wondered if he'd got cold feet at the thought of being tied to her for ever. Or had he thought her unattractive? Overweight? Not good in bed? Found another woman? All the insecurities she'd learned to deal with now flashed up in her head, but she quickly shoved them away. She was at work, not the place to be thinking about the past.

'Blenheim One departing Wairau ED, en route to Base.' His tone was measured, professional as he relayed details to Coms. It was the voice he used to calm distraught patients before he started gently teasing them and making them smile. The times she'd seen him on the wards he'd been completely at ease with patients and their families, making them feel they'd had his undivided attention for as long as they'd needed it.

'Did you finish your medical degree?' The words were out before she could stop them.

'No.' His fingers whitened as they pushed the handset back onto its hook.

'Why not? All you ever wanted to be was a doctor. Even when we were kids you'd tell everyone that's what you were going to be when you grew up.'

'I changed my mind.'

Stunned, she again spoke without thinking, 'You changed your mind after four years of study? Why?'

'I wasn't ready.'

'Not ready? For what? You loved medicine. I remember all those endless nights you put in studying and not begrudging a single second. You couldn't wait to get to university or the hospital every morning to learn more. You loved it all. There was the day you came home shouting with excitement, saying you wanted to be a surgeon, that surgery was amazing. Then months later you decided paediatrics was the greatest, all those little kids needing your care. Then—'

'Drop it,' Fraser snapped at her. 'Just leave it, will you?' The eyes he turned to her glittered angrily. His fists pounded his thighs. 'I had a change of heart, Nik. That's all.'

Perversely *her* heart swelled. He'd called her Nik, his pet name for her. No one else dared call her Nik. Until Fraser she'd hated it. Had he used it to drive his point home? Or because he still cared a little about her?

Idiot. Even if he does, it means nothing. You're not interested in getting back with him, only in finding out why he took off in such a flaming hurry without a word of explanation.

Nothing had changed in that respect. He'd made it very clear he had no intention of telling her anything about what he'd been up to in the intervening years. She needed to mind her own business, even with Fraser. But she'd like some closure, even after all this time.

The radio squawked to life. 'Blenheim One, stand by.'

Snatching up the handset, Fraser acknowledged, 'Roger, Blenheim One standing by.' His relief at the diversion throbbed between them.

Nikki pulled the ambulance over to the side of the road to wait until they found out where they were needed next. Her fingers drummed on the steering-wheel as she waited for the details. Her stomach cramped as it squeezed around yet more disappointment about Fraser. The silence between them was heavy with all the things they'd left unsaid. Had he ever really loved her? Had he got caught up in the excitement of their relationship and popped the question without thinking the ramifications through? Unlike her. She'd always loved Fraser, had always wanted to marry him and have his babies. She shot a quick glance in his direction, saw his face in profile as he glared outside, his chin pushed forward, the corner of his mouth white with tension.

'Blenheim One, male, nineteen years old, severe abdo pain,' the dispatcher intoned over the radio, her voice sharp in the frosty air of the cab.

Thank goodness. With a patient to deal with they could forget everything else for a while. Forget? Or postpone?

'Roger, Coms.' Fraser tapped the screen to bring up the patient details.

Nikki noted the address and made a U-turn, making a mental list of the obs she'd do for a patient with abdominal pain.

Fraser appeared fascinated with the passing houses. Then he surprised her further. 'I'm not the only one to change careers. You always talked of being a chef, and had a goal to work in a top-class restaurant. What happened to that, Nikki?'

He'd turned the tables on her. She turned them back. 'I never went back to Dunedin after you dumped me. I quit my job and stayed at home on the farm.' She'd never have survived returning to the city where they'd lived. 'You must've noticed that much.'

His mouth tightened. Regretting asking about her past now? 'Who do you think packed up all your gear from our flat and sent it up to your parents' farm?'

She deflated like a balloon suddenly let go. 'I never knew it was you. I just thought it would've been one of our friends.' So it had been Fraser who'd put into one of the boxes her favourite photo of them together at St Kilda beach. It now lay at the back of the wardrobe in her old room at the farm. 'Did you leave university then? Or later?'

He ducked that one. 'What made you choose the ambulance service?'

She sighed. 'Dad had an accident, rolled the tractor at the back of the farm. Luckily he was thrown clear but still copped a broken femur and a punctured lung.' Nikki paused, reliving the scene she'd come across when her dad hadn't come in for lunch on time. 'At first I thought he was dying, he looked so still and pale. I freaked.' She'd wished Fraser had been there because he'd have known what to do.

Fraser had turned to look at her. 'A frightening situation.'

'Terrifying. The ambulance crew were fantastic and I began to see something else I might consider doing for a job. I volunteered the next week and gave them every hour I had free.' It had also made her feel closer to him—for a while.

'But you always hated the sight of blood.' Fraser shook his head.

'I got over that really fast.'

'But you gave up your passion. I remember those fantastic meals you created. There was never a time when there wasn't something tasty in our fridge. Our friends used to draw straws to see who came to dinner in our cramped flat because you loved giving them gastronomically divine treats…' His voice trailed off. 'Oh.'

'Exactly.' There hadn't been a lot of fun in

cooking after they'd broken up. Cooking was her way of expressing love and friendship, and for a long while she had struggled with the whole concept. She'd got a job as junior chef at one of Blenheim's vineyard restaurants but it had been a drag, a way of earning an income, not a lot of fun. Because her passion for food had disappeared.

Moments later Fraser said, 'Here's our stop. That narrow driveway by the hedge. You'll have to park on the roadside.' He stood and pushed through to the back, no doubt to get the pack. His hip brushed her shoulder lightly.

She braked sharply. Sucked air through her teeth. It was only a hip. An unintentional touch.

'Hey,' Fraser called out.

'Sorry,' she muttered, and eased the heavy vehicle alongside the pavement. She was toast if she went hyper every time Fraser inadvertently bumped against her, because it was going to happen often working together with a patient in the crowded confines of the ambulance. She shoved her door wide, dropped to the ground with a thud, jarring her teeth. Not even halfway through day one of his training and she was going stark raving bonkers with emotions all over the place.

A girl aged in her late teens let them into the untidy house. 'Col's in a lot of pain. He can't move at all.'

Nikki followed her through to the lounge, trying not to breathe deeply as the rancid stench of body odour swamped her nostrils. Looking for a clean spot to put down the pack, she asked the young man sprawled across the couch, 'Col Hargreaves? I'm Nikki. I hear you've got a pain in your stomach.' She had to shout over the din from the enormous television.

'It's agony,' the man groaned.

'Can you show me exactly where it's hurting?' Nikki crouched down beside the couch and, picking up the remote, lowered the noise level.

Tugging his sweatshirt up, Col stabbed the right side of his belly with his forefinger. 'Here.' Another poke on the left side. 'And here.'

'How long has this been going on?'

'Since last night.' Col moved sideways and foul language followed.

Wrapping the pressure cuff around his upper arm, Nikki kept up the questions, trying to ignore everything else. 'Have you had something like this before?'

'Yeah, last week. Your lot took me to hospital but the doctor couldn't find what was wrong. Are you going to take me there again?'

'Yes, after we've taken some readings.' She wrote the normal blood pressure results on her glove. 'What were you doing when the pain started?' She could hear Fraser pushing the stretcher through the door behind her.

'Watching TV.' Her patient gave a loud and drawn-out groan. 'I get giddy too. Ahh,' he squealed.

'Take it easy. On a scale of one to ten how strong is the pain?'

'Ten.'

Then he should be writhing in agony. 'Is it hurting anywhere else?'

'Nah, only in my gut.'

'Okay, Col. We need to get you up onto the stretcher. Reckon you can do that by yourself?'

'Lady, I'm in pain here.'

Fraser stepped around the stretcher. 'Right, bud, we'll take an arm each to help you up. On the count of three, ready?' When Col grunted,

Fraser continued, 'One, two three.' And he hauled the guy upright.

Nikki helped get Col onto the stretcher and covered him with a blanket. She had a shrewd suspicion Col was more than able to walk out to the ambulance if he had a mind to. His symptoms were hard to pin down and he'd groaned before she'd touched his stomach, making her suspicious about what he was up to. But she could be very wrong. They'd make Col's shift to their vehicle as comfortable as possible.

Fraser pressed the stretcher's brake off and pushed the stretcher out to the ambulance. 'We'll soon have you in ED and the doctors can check you over.'

'What about my girlfriend? She's got to come.'

Col's belligerence was beginning to annoy Nikki but she offered a lift to the girl and indicated the front seat. The trip to the hospital was punctuated with loud groans and intermittent swearing.

After handing Col over to the ED staff, Fraser commented dryly, 'That guy bounced across from the stretcher to the hospital bed. What happened to the level-ten pain? He's having everyone on.'

'Not our problem any more. But maybe he needs someone to take notice of him, for whatever reason.' She stepped into the back of the ambulance. 'You drive. I'm going to wipe down the stretcher with antiseptic and see if I can't get rid of that overpowering stink of sweat.' It had taken over their vehicle.

What she wouldn't give for a shower and a clean uniform. She began scrubbing every surface she could. Funny how that particular odour hung around long after the cause had gone.

Nikki's cellphone rang as Fraser backed into the garage bay back at Base. Flipping it open, she smiled. It was Jay, her big, bad brother, who'd recently joined a rural vet practice close to the farm they'd grown up on. Nearly two years older than her, he was the youngest of her four brothers. He'd also been Fraser's best friend at one time. Jay had taken it almost as hard as she had when Fraser had gone away. 'Morning—'

'Did I just see McCall in the ambulance with you?' Jay's deep voice rumbled in her ear.

It had taken all of two hours for the news to

get out, quite slow for Blenheim. 'Yes, the one and only.'

'What's he doing here? When did he return?'

The ambulance stopped and Nikki quickly slipped away to head outside the garage. This was one conversation she didn't want Fraser overhearing. 'I only found out last week when Mike told us he'd got a job here.'

'He's not working as your partner, is he?'

'Yeah, Jay, he is. It's not like I had a choice. Believe me, I tried to get out of it but Mike insisted we work together.'

'Work together? What's this about? Why would a doctor want to work on the ambulances?'

'Thanks, Jay. Our job isn't for the brain dead.'

'I know that.' Jay paused then went on, 'So what's going on? Is McCall here for a week? Or for ever?'

'I'm not sure. Definitely more than a week.' She quickly filled Jay in about Fraser's father, before telling him, 'Fraser didn't finish med school.'

'No way! He was destined for a great career. No, sis, you've got it wrong.'

'He told me himself.'

'Did he say why?'

'You think he would?'

'I think he should,' Jay growled. 'So he's still hiding things from you. Wait till I see him. It's time he knew exactly how we all feel about him.'

She surprised herself by saying, 'Jay, leave him alone for now. Give him a chance. Who knows? He might turn up at the farm one day with a six pack of lager under his arm and apologise to us all for the trouble he caused.'

'Sis, if you believe that, then you believe in the tooth fairy.'

Fraser plugged the electricity source into the ambulance, wincing as Nikki's words reached him. He was going to have to move a lot faster than he'd intended. Apologising to the Page family was on his latest to-do list. Only he'd figured it wise to first let them get used to the fact he was back.

But if Jay was on the case he'd be breaking down his mum and dad's front door by sundown tonight. The Page men were known to be very protective of their sister. Especially Jay, who carried his own demons about the sister who'd drowned years ago.

Fraser drew a deep breath. Gawd, he'd missed Jay. They'd done a lot together—getting into trouble as teens, surviving their first hangovers, learning to drive, racing motorbikes on the Page farm, playing in the school first fifteen and the cricket team. So much of his wonderful life and friendships back then had been tied up with Nikki's family. All had gone down the gurgler because he hadn't known how to handle the terrifying situation he'd suddenly found himself thrown into five years ago.

When the garage door rattled downwards Fraser realised Nikki had finished her phone call and was standing beside him. 'Are you happy with the way those callouts went?' she asked, one hand on her hip.

'Absolutely. So far everything works the same way it does in Dunedin.'

'Good. Do you know when you'll be starting your courses?'

'Online workshops start in a couple of weeks and my first week away in Christchurch is next month.'

Nikki was deliberately showing him that their relationship was strictly professional. He'd have gone along with that if she hadn't discussed him with Jay.

Tonight. Tonight he'd visit Nikki and lay the past to rest. A cold sweat broke out on his brow. All those years and he still wasn't prepared for her reaction to what he had to tell her. He did not want to see pity in her eyes. He did not want sympathy. He just wanted a clear conscience.

Tonight. After they knocked off for the day. He'd get her address and pay her a visit.

CHAPTER THREE

'WHY are we doing a Life Flight pick-up?' Fraser negotiated the ambulance through the lunchtime traffic the next day. 'Surely two paramedics for this job is overkill?'

'Blenheim Two's already out on a job so there's no one else.' Nikki didn't look up from her paperwork. 'But if there's a priority one call we'll ditch the pick-up.'

Fraser rubbed his aching head. Another sleepless night tossing and turning after his plan to see Nikki had gone awry. He'd wheedled Nikki's address out of Amber when she'd come on for the night shift and had headed straight around there, only to find the place in darkness. He'd returned after dinner with his parents but Nikki still hadn't come home so he'd had no choice but to forget about talking to her last night. But he would try again tonight, and every night until she was at home and ready to listen to him.

As he drove down Middle Renwick Road towards the airport, they passed row after row after row of grapevines, some still being pruned. 'The vines always look naked at this time of year. I'd forgotten how I always knew the season by the vines and the activities in the vineyards.' A pang of homesickness struck Fraser, despite being back here. This was one of the things he'd come back to Blenheim for, he suddenly realised. A sigh trickled past his lips. He was home physically, but in any other respect he had a long way to go.

'Remember when it used to be cherry and apricot orchards, and paddocks filled with carrots and peas that you drove past.' Nikki glanced out at the passing scenery.

'Not many of those left now. I heard that the council rates have been driven up with all the vineyards creating high prices for the land.'

'Yep, and that's a sore point with some of the older farmers.' Nikki touched the icons on the screen in front of her. 'Our patient's been having chemo and radiation in Wellington. Bowel cancer.'

'Ouch.' An old, familiar tug of horror and fear

grabbed at Fraser. The fear that had receded over the years since his treatment still managed to raise its ugly head at times to twist his gut. Like a warning not to get too complacent as it could come back. But, no, it would not. Must not.

Nikki continued reading aloud. 'Glen Wright. Twenty years old. Hell, that's terrible. He's so young. How does someone deal with that? He's got his whole life ahead of him.'

You have no idea. Fraser pressed his mouth tight, kept the words in. Now was definitely not the moment to be revealing his secret. Gawd, if Nik had been at home last night she'd know the answers to her questions.

She hadn't finished. 'I hope he's got a good prognosis. At twenty he'll have hardly done a thing with his life.'

Nope, he won't have. But he sure as hell will hurry on with it the moment he's fit enough. 'It must've been dreadful for him to learn he had cancer.'

It would've blown the guy's mind wide apart with fear and disbelief and shock. It would've stopped him eating and sleeping for days. He'd have looked out at the world with a deep longing for all that he could be deprived of. He'd wonder what he'd done so wrong to be thrown into this situation.

'You planning on snapping that steering-wheel?' Nikki's eyebrows rose cutely.

'Not today.' He tried to relax his fingers and his brain. A return mental trip to those bleak days would achieve absolutely nothing but darkness. And the darkness was over. With the all-clear, he'd been given a fresh start on life, which he mustn't waste.

Stopping at the security gate leading onto the tarmac, he punched in the access code Nikki reeled off and watched the gate slowly pull back. 'I called round to see you last night.'

Nikki jerked around in her seat, her beautiful azure eyes darkening with worry, panic even. 'Why? I thought we agreed to keep everything on a professional level.'

Why had he opened his goddamned mouth? Now he'd have to give her some reason or she'd niggle away at him all day to find out what he'd wanted to see her about. The truth but nowhere near the whole truth? 'Thought we might discuss how we're going to make this crewing together work without too much aggro.'

'We can do that on the job.' She wasn't giving him any leeway. 'Move, or the gate will close on us again.'

Fraser blinked. When had the gate opened fully?

Pointing to the left, Nikki told him, 'Keep your speed at ten k's an hour and park between that hangar and the painted circle on the tarmac.'

Easing the ambulance onto the edge of the tarmac, he watched the plane rolling along the taxiway, the wintery sun highlighting its bright red paintwork. Beyond the flat ground of the airport the rolling curves and sharp edges of the Wither Hills wore their winter green.

Fraser dropped down onto the tarmac, asked over his shoulder, 'What's our role here?'

'We help transfer the patient and drive him to hospital. He's accompanied by two nurses, who take care of him. They'll return to their plane by taxi once they've handed over to the ward staff.'

'That's it?'

Nik came around the front of the truck and looked up at him. 'Guess you never had to do this in Dunedin where there's a big hospital with all the bells and whistles. Unfortunately there are many instances when local patients are sent away for major surgery or treatment. These flights save them an awful lot of discomfort getting home.'

The sound of the engines of the advancing plane drowned out anything else she might have said. As soon as the props stopped spinning a side door popped open and an elevator with a platform attached began sliding out.

Nikki told him, 'You can move the truck closer now. Come from the back. The pilot gets antsy if he thinks his wingtip is in jeopardy.'

Yes, boss. Keep it professional. Absolutely. Fraser felt a wry smile tugging his lips. 'On my way.'

He'd barely braked to a halt when Nikki had the back doors open and the stretcher out. A chill wind edged under the collar of his thick uniform jacket, making him shiver. 'The sooner Glen's inside the ambulance the better.' The guy's resistance to the cold would be low if he'd just finished a round of chemo. Fraser shivered, this time not from the cold but from the melancholy memories of his own chemical-ravaged body in the days after treatment.

On the platform at the plane's side was a stretcher with Glen strapped on. He was looking around with dull, tired eyes, barely acknowledging what was going on.

'Hey, Glen, you're nearly home,' one of the nurses dressed in blue overalls commented.

'Sure,' the guy muttered.

'Hospital ain't home, is it?' Fraser gave Glen a knowing smile.

Glen's eyelids lifted. 'You're damned right, mate.'

'Let's get you out of the wind.' Fraser snapped buckles together to keep their patient from moving. With Glen quickly installed inside the vehicle, Fraser slid behind the steering-wheel and eased the vehicle forward, vowing to make the trip as smooth and bump-free as possible. *As you do every trip.*

Yeah, but this one's special.

Nikki had just added the mussels to her paella when the door chime rang. She dropped the wooden spoon and rice splattered over the stovetop. 'Dang. Who's calling at dinnertime?'

Her heart stuttered. Not Fraser, surely? He'd been around last night when she'd been out at the movies. Unfortunately Amber, sensing something going on between Fraser and her, had been quick to give him their address.

Another ring from the door. 'All right, hold on.' She swung the front door wide. And leaned against the doorjamb as casually as tight nerves and shaking hands allowed. 'Fraser. I thought we'd agreed to keep work at work.' Talking was difficult with a mouth as dry as dust.

'A six pack of lager, I think you said.' Fraser held the pack out.

'You overheard me talking to Jay yesterday.' And she'd have to find a tooth to put under her pillow for the fairy.

'But if you're not into lager then I've got this.' In his other hand was a bottle of very good Chardonnay. 'Not knowing what you drink these days, I'm covering my options.'

'You need me on side that much? Is this where you tell me why you didn't turn up for our wedding?' Gripping the edge of the door, she held herself upright through sheer determination. She'd wanted to know this for ever and yet now she shook with nerves. She could learn bad stuff that would shatter her carefully restored confidence.

'Nik, let me in.' His tone was gentle. 'Please.'

Every time he called her Nik she softened towards him. Did he know that? Was that why he used her pet name? Sucking in her stomach and straightening her back, she waved him inside and shut the door. Shut Fraser inside with her. Too late to say no now. She breathed in the tang of lime aftershave and regretted her capitulation. Anything to do with Fraser always became too hard too quickly. So much for remaining calm, aloof, non-involved. It wasn't possible whenever he came near.

So she would hear him out and move on. Then maybe she'd even manage to be happy working with him. As she pushed past him in the narrow hall, her arm slid over his, but she clamped down on the instant surge of longing that contact brought.

A strong burning smell. 'The risotto,' she screeched, and raced into the kitchen to snatch the deep pan off the gas ring. 'Great, there goes my dinner.'

Fraser peered around her at the risotto. 'Can't you lift off the top layer carefully? It'll only be burned on the bottom.' His tongue did a lap of his lips. 'It looks damned good from here.'

She raised her gaze to glare at him. 'Help yourself.'

A wee smile lurked at the corners of his mouth. 'You're not afraid I'll tell everyone you served me burned food? That could ruin your reputation as a great cook.'

'If you're talking about the gang at work they'll ignore you for fear they won't get their weekly quota of home-made cakes and biscuits.'

'True. The way to anyone's heart is through their stomach.' Fraser put down the wine and beer and scooped up a mouthful of risotto with the wooden spoon.

She watched as the spoon slipped into his mouth, saw his tongue clear the rice off the wooden surface. She leant against the bench for support. For the second time in two days desire spread through her like wildfire, heating her in long-chilled places, suffocating her in need.

Heaven help her, it was only paella, and yet the guy made it the sexiest food out.

'Divine. A little smoky but absolutely delicious.' He took another spoonful, his eyes rolling and that tentative smile growing.

Resignedly, Nikki found a plate and a fork, handed them to him. 'Help yourself.' Tugging a bottle from the six pack, she twisted the cap off and took a long, cold drink. It cooled her throat, but nothing else. Why had she opened her front door so wide and invited Fraser in? This had not been what she'd expected, this deep need clawing its way down her body, teasing her, taunting her.

Bang. The bottom of the bottle cracked on the bench as she put it down. 'Come on, let's get this over with.' Her voice came out light and squeaky. Clearing her throat, she tried again. 'Why are you here, Fraser?'

The fork that had been about to slide into his mouth stopped, held still as Fraser studied her frankly, closely, for a long time. Like he was looking for something.

'What?' Goose-bumps lifted on her skin in

foreboding as she saw the sorrow and trepidation begin filtering into his eyes.

Finally, Fraser dropped the fork back onto the plate and pushed it all aside. He turned away, stared around the kitchen/dinning room, turned back to her. His chest lifted as he drew a breath.

Nikki began to shake. This was nothing like the breezy 'I'm sorry' she'd expected. This was serious. 'You're frightening me.'

'I had cancer.'

She gasped. Her Fraser had cancer. Fear bounded through her, turned her legs to jelly, made her head swirl, her hands open and close, open and close. Reaching for the closest chair, she hauled it near, dropped down onto it.

'Are…?' She swallowed, tried again. 'Are you all right?' Dumb, dumb question. As if. He's got cancer, idiot. Of course he's not all right. He could be dying. Never in a million years had she imagined anything so dreadful, so terrifying. Deep shudders racked her. Nausea rose, soured her mouth. Fraser? Cancer? Oh, no. It couldn't be true. It mustn't be.

'I'm fine now.'

'What?' She blinked at him. How could he

sound so calm? Didn't he understand how serious cancer was?

She told herself to get a grip. If anyone in this room knew the answer to that it was Fraser. He'd been there.

He straddled the chair opposite, propping his hands on its back. 'I *had* cancer. It's gone. The all-clear came through last month.'

Relief poured through her. She slumped farther down her chair. Fraser was fine. Not sick, not dying. He was as healthy as he looked. Phew. Her shaky hand brushed over her banging heart. It was all right. Fraser was going to make it. She lifted her gaze to his face. Saw again the new lines around his mouth, the seriousness in his eyes. Now she understood the change in his hair. 'You had chemo.' When hair grew back after that treatment it could be a different colour and sometimes it turned curly.

'And radiation,' he told her.

Hang on. 'It takes five years for an all-clear.' She couldn't focus on one thing at a time as she struggled to take it all in.

Sadness filled his eyes, turned his mouth down. 'Yes, it does.'

'So, around our wedding date?'

He understood her question. 'Three weeks before.'

'Three weeks?' The air hissed out of her lungs. The old, familiar pain of humiliation slammed into her. How could he not have wanted her there with him? Not wanted to share his pain with her? 'Why didn't you tell me?' she whispered.

'I mucked up. Big time. But you have to believe me when I say I thought I was doing the right thing. For you. For us.' Fraser shoved off the chair, strode to the window to stare out into the night. 'It was incredibly difficult. I had testicular cancer. I struggled to deal with it myself, let alone tell anyone else. Especially you.'

Her eyes squeezed shut. A new pain clutched at her. Pain for Fraser. Any cancer was bad, but for some reason this seemed worse. She couldn't explain it but knew it was all tied up with his virility, his very essence. He'd been a sexual man, enjoyed making love. What man didn't? But this had happened to Fraser, her Fraser.

'Why especially me?'

He reached for the wine bottle. 'Got a glass?'

She found two, put them on the table and returned to her seat, still trying to get her head around this nightmare.

Fraser filled both glasses, pushed one towards her. 'I was afraid that you'd leave me, that you'd find excuses because I was no longer the man you'd loved. Often I tried to ring you but every time I picked up the phone and dialled I'd hear you in my mind telling me you wanted no part of it so I'd hang up before you answered.'

The wine was cool and beautiful on her tongue. Swallowing, she pushed the glass aside. It was out of place at the moment. 'So you got in first and left me.' She squeezed her eyes tight. He hadn't had a lot of trust in her love, then.

'Nikki,' he called softly. 'It wasn't like that. Believe me.'

Slowly, she opened her eyes and looked at him. Really looked, looking for the man he'd become, not the man she'd thought she still knew. And her heart broke again. For them both. So much had happened, things they should've shared and hadn't. Of course her depression didn't compare to his, and it probably wouldn't have happened if she'd known the truth behind him leaving her.

Fraser should have told her, no matter how hard it would have been.

'You went away without a word. That short phone call was hardly an explanation.'

She'd still had to face people, return their gifts, pack up her wedding gown, eat the food already prepared and paid for and delivered to her parents' home. And the whole time the tears had kept sliding down her face, soaking into her clothes, exhausting her.

He came back to the chair, sat opposite her and reached for her hands. 'I am so sorry for how I treated you, for what I did.' His fingers were trembling as they squeezed her hands. 'When I heard about the cancer I was terrified. I thought I'd been given a sentence. There was so much to think about and my mind was such a mess I was completely unable to make the right decisions. And I didn't want your pity.'

'As if.' Another thought hit her. 'Was I in Dunedin when you found out?'

He shook his head. 'I found out three days after you left to come up here to sort out all the last-minute things for the wedding. I'd been tired and irritable but put it down to all the study and exams, and our upcoming wedding. But after falling asleep on duty one night I decided to see a doctor to get a prescription for something to give me some energy. I got more than I'd bargained for.'

She pulled a face at the thought. Her skin felt clammy. Her stomach quaked at the fear for him. 'Finding out must've been horrible.' On his own. 'I could've been with you.'

'I didn't even know the doctor had asked for a PSA test. He'd only ticked the boxes for anaemia on the blood test request form. Apparently, he rang the lab and added the prostate test as an afterthought. Damn him.'

When Nikki raised her eyebrows, he added, 'It's kind of like the ostrich syndrome. If the doc hadn't asked for the test I'd never have known I had cancer and therefore it wouldn't have existed.'

'Yeah, sure.'

'Very scientific, I know.' Fraser squeezed her hands and put them back in her lap. 'It's a big ask but I hope one day you can forgive me.' The glass he lifted to his lips was unsteady. One mouthful and half the wine had gone. 'The oncologist told me I had to have surgery urgently, followed by chemo and radiation. He also mentioned that I'd be sterile after that treatment.'

'Oh, Fraser. I'd have coped with that. It was you I wanted, loved, not any future children.'

'Nikki, Nikki.' He shook his head again. 'You loved kids, always made jokes about having a dozen. Your own cricket team with a reserve, you used to quip. How could I take that away from you?'

'How about letting me make up my own mind about it? Huh? Ever think of that? I'm not denying it would've been disappointing but nothing in comparison to what losing you was like. I wasn't marrying you to have children. I wanted to spend my life with you because I loved you.'

'I did have my sperm frozen for later, but it felt all wrong to be asking you to deal with that at the time.'

'Easier to leave me on the day of my wedding?' The bitterness was unexpected and wrong. Fraser had been through hell and it didn't matter how badly he'd treated her. He deserved better. Who knew how they'd have dealt with his situation unless they'd faced it?

Ashamed, she glanced across. 'Sorry, that was

uncalled for. You must've been going through hell. I only wish I'd known. That's what relationships are about—sharing the good and the bad. I'd have been with you the whole way through, fighting for you when you didn't have the strength, boosting your morale when you didn't think you'd make it. That's what my love for you meant.' Tears streamed down her cheeks, but she ignored them. 'I'd have done anything for you back then.'

He stood up, ran a hand over her head, down her cheek, cupped her chin. His eyes were deep, anguished pools, not brown, not black, a nothing dark shade of despair. 'Exactly. I couldn't handle that.'

Then he was gone, closing the front door quietly behind him. Leaving her shocked and shivering. With questions crashing around her skull. Sadness mixed with anger. Self-righteousness laced with despair. And seeping through it all a dawning understanding of the man she'd once loved more than life itself.

Fraser walked along the edge of the Taylor River where it meandered through town. His hands were shoved into the pockets of his trousers, his chin almost touching his chest. His mind held an image of Nikki opening the door, dressed in designer, hip-hugging jeans and a fluffy blue sweater the colour of her eyes. Stunned at how gorgeous she'd looked, he'd struggled not to haul her into his arms and kiss her. Temptation in clothes.

Then the other images overtook him. The images he'd expected right from the beginning. Her shock at his revelation. The sadness, the fear. Her anger at him for not sharing the news with her back at the beginning.

Nikki owned his heart. She always had. At some time between being a kid and turning into a teenager he'd fallen in love with his best friend's sister. She'd stolen his breath away with her easy smile and twinkling eyes, her cute nose and smattering of freckles. Only as he'd grown up had he learned that those feelings swamping him were all to do with love.

She'd hated those freckles and covered them with a hefty layer of make-up whenever she could. And nowadays the smile and twinkle had gone. Because of him?

He'd effectively killed her love. But he'd saved her a load of anguish. While he regretted how he'd broken off with her, he couldn't regret doing it. For her sake. He'd loved her too much to ever ask her to give up her dreams for him. And now? When he was home, ready to pick up his life?

Now was too late. For him and Nik. She'd moved on, made a life that would never include him. She'd become totally self-sufficient, self-reliant. She didn't need him. He didn't need her. Right? Right.

Loud laughter had him snapping his head up, gazing at the restaurant that stood at the top of the bank overlooking the river. People sat around tables, enjoying themselves, each other, sharing meals and wine. Surprised at the longing gripping him, he hesitated. He'd missed that kind of intimacy ever since he'd left Nikki. Not even his close friends had filled the gap made by her absence. Neither had the parade of forgettable women he'd been with to test himself, to assess the true level of his loss, to try to blank out his past.

If this was his new life then he was damned if he'd stand on the outside looking in and feeling sorry for himself. Striding up the steps, he entered the restaurant and took a seat at the bar, ordering a glass of cabernet merlot and a rare steak from a passing waitress.

'Hey, Fraser McCall, is that you?' The barman placed the wine in front of him.

Fraser studied the man on the other side of the counter before shoving his hand out. 'Mark Stevens, how the hell are you, man?'

'Heard you were back in town. On the ambulances, aren't you? With Nikki. You two got together again? That's great news.'

Ouch. The reality of small towns, home, was that everyone thought they knew your business. 'No, we're only working together.'

'Aw, shucks, man. I couldn't believe it when I heard you'd split. Everyone knew you were made for each other.'

Fraser swirled the wine in the glass, tasted it, nodding his approval for the wine, not for the way the conversation had gone. Maybe he should've kept walking. Walking away from life? 'So, Mark, what about you? I see you're wearing a wedding ring. Who's the lucky woman?'

He was home, with all that entailed. Tonight

he'd apologised to Nikki. Two steps forward. And Mark had underscored what his own heart knew but had recovered from—Nik and he had belonged together. One step back.

CHAPTER FOUR

'THIS one's yours,' Nikki told Fraser as they responded to a priority call. Being a mentor had its benefits. By putting Fraser in charge of the job she could observe his techniques. And keep him busy so he wouldn't have time to talk about anything other than work.

'Sure thing.' Fraser looked up from the PRF he held, as though waiting for her to say more. When she didn't, he began filling in details on the page.

Dang, she was tired. If she'd got five minutes' sleep last night, she'd have been lucky. Fraser's words, all of them, had gone round and round and round in her mind until finally just before 4:00 a.m. she'd got up and made a hot chocolate and watched mindless TV, crying for Fraser and what he must've been through, until Amber had come in a little after six.

It was shift changeover day, which meant

Nikki and Fraser had had the day off in preparation for working the next two nights. Nikki had skulked around the flat most of the day, venturing out for her run late in the morning. Her head had ached so much her skull had felt as though it would split in half and she'd returned home after only twenty minutes, deciding ibuprofen and a hot shower were more likely to set her up for work than running for an hour. Tomorrow, she'd make up for the lost kilometres.

A car pulled out from the kerb directly in front of the ambulance, forcing her to brake hard. Her hand slammed the auxiliary horn. 'Moron. Can't you hear the siren? We're right behind you.'

'Their stereo's probably heaving.' Fraser read aloud, '"John Gemmell, male, twenty-nine, fell out of a tree."'

'What was he doing up a tree in the dark?' she snapped. 'It's after seven o'clock. Got to be nuts.'

Fraser outlined his approach to the call they were attending. 'I'm thinking there could be spinal and or head injuries, fractured limbs. Depending on whether the guy landed on flat ground or obstacles lying around he could also have internal injuries.'

'Yes.' He knew all that, so why run it by her? Making conversation? As she sped down Renwick Road she tried not to think any more about his revelations from the previous evening. There was nothing to be gained by it, but it was very hard to stop considering all the ramifications.

'Two hundred metres to Jackson's Road,' Fraser intoned.

That golden voice reminded her of things she didn't want to remember. Whispers of sweet nothings that had led to kisses to die for. Kisses that had led to exquisite love-making. Her hands tightened on the steering-wheel while her tongue slid across her lips. Disturbing when she was actually angry at him.

Fraser peered through the gloom. 'Looks like that's the place. Plenty of lights on. According to Coms there's a small track we're to follow next door to the winery entrance.'

'Right.' Nikki focused entirely on navigating the wide vehicle down the narrow, rutted driveway, finally reaching a ramshackle cottage where lights blazed through the dark. After lots of negotiating backwards and forwards in the small area, with a woman who'd been waiting for them on the porch directing her, she got the truck backed around and ready for an easy departure.

Hopping out, she snapped on gloves and asked, 'Where's Mr Gemmell?'

'Around the other side of the house,' the woman told her. 'He's bad, not moving and groaning all the time.'

'We'll check him over before taking him into hospital,' Nikki said.

'My sister, John's wife, is with him. You might need to give her something to calm down as well.'

'Hopefully she'll feel better when we've got John in the ambulance,' Nikki said quietly as she reached for the stretcher at the same time as Fraser. Her hand snagged on his. Snatching her hand away, she kept her face blank, hoping the flare of heat cooking her brain wasn't warming her cheeks.

'Want to show me the way?' Fraser asked the woman, and headed around the side of the house without a backward glance.

'He wasn't affected at all. Which means he doesn't have any residual feelings for you.' Nikki muttered to herself as she pulled the stretcher free, letting its wheels fall to the ground so she could lock them in place. 'Not that you want to go down the Fraser track again either.' He might've had a very plausible explanation for his desertion but she'd never completely trust him again. No way. And without trust she had nothing.

Placing the backboard and a collar on the stretcher, she headed in the direction Fraser had gone, looking for hazards on her way. At least headlights from a parked car lit up the area, making it easier to see.

Fraser was asking, 'Is John conscious?'

'Yes, has been all the time.'

'How long ago did he fall?' Fraser unzipped his bag.

'It must be nearly an hour. He went outside to feed the dogs and when he didn't come back after a few minutes I went looking for him,' the woman who'd met them replied.

'Are the dogs tied up?' he asked, glancing around.

'Yes.'

'Why did he climb the tree?' Nikki pushed the

stretcher to the side, out of the way until they were ready to shift John.

'It wasn't a tree. He came off the roof and crashed through the fence,' the woman explained.

'Sorry, we've been given the wrong details.'

'He'd been muttering about tomorrow's predicted frost freezing the pipes. The lagging came off in the wind yesterday so he climbed up to tie it back.'

Glancing upwards, Nikki could see the corrugated iron gleaming with moisture. The sky was clear, the stars twinkling through the freezing air. It wouldn't be long before ice began forming.

Fraser introduced himself to the man sprawled on his back on a muddy patch of long grass and covered in blankets. Beside him knelt a thin young woman, gripping his hand so hard his bones were in danger of more trauma. 'He's real bad,' she gasped.

'John, are you in any pain?' Fraser asked.

'My head hurts, and my leg and back.' John's voice was very soft and Fraser had to lean close to hear him.

'On a scale of one to ten, ten being the worst, how bad is the pain in your head?'

John murmured, 'Bad. Eight.'

'And your leg and back?' Fraser continued his visual appraisal of John.

'Leg ten,' John gasped as he inadvertently tried to shift his legs. 'Back five.'

'Okay, John, I'll give you something for the pain in a moment. I just need to run my hands over your body, checking everywhere for injuries you might not be aware of,' Fraser continued. 'Try not to move your head. We'll put a collar on shortly as a safety measure.' Beginning at the head, Fraser began examining John thoroughly.

Nikki eased close beside the woman on the opposite side. 'I'm Nikki. Are you John's wife?'

'Yes. My name's Alison.'

'Okay, Alison, can I get you to move a bit so I can reach John? There are some tests I have to do.' She noted the smell of alcohol on John's breath as she pushed up his jersey and undid his shirt. How could anyone even think about clambering onto a slippery roof after having had alcohol? But all she said was, 'John, I'm going to take your pulse and heart rate.'

'Pulse is weak, Glasgow coma scale is ten,' Nikki soon told Fraser, meaning that John was responding moderately well to their questions with speech and eye contact, and was reacting to pain by withdrawing from any stimuli. 'Mild hypothermia, too.'

'Not surprising. It's freezing out here,' Fraser acknowledged. 'Fractured lower leg. Possibly tib and fib.'

As Fraser gently worked his hands down John's left leg his patient cried out and then swore. 'Sorry,' John muttered a minute later. 'I didn't mean to curse you. It's just that it's bloody painful.'

Nikki unzipped her drugs bag. 'Let's give you some morphine for starters. That'll help ease the pain.' The defibrillator printed out some figures. 'Blood pressure mildly elevated. Oxygen saturation still at eighty-five per cent.'

When they'd got the plastic collar around John's neck Fraser hunkered down where he could be seen by John without him having to move at all. 'We're going splint your lower leg to prevent movement when we slide you onto a board. Even with the morphine it's going to hurt a bit, I'm afraid. If the pain's too bad tell us and we'll give you a suck on the Entonox.'

'What's Entonox?' Mary asked.

'Laughing gas.' Fraser was handling the situation perfectly.

Nikki's mouth dried. He was so good at anything he set his mind to. Even at shutting her out. That hurt. A lot. Now that she'd got past the shock of him having cancer, other emotions were taking over.

Disbelief that she hadn't sensed something was so wrong, hadn't noticed he hadn't been well. Could all the excitement and preparations of the wedding have dominated her mind so much she hadn't been taking any notice of the man she was supposed to marry?

Resentment and anger at not being trusted with Fraser's own fear, at not being allowed to support him or make decisions with him about their future.

'On the count of three.' Fraser nudged her attention back to their patient.

With John sucking gas, they carefully rolled

him onto his right side and slid the board as far under him as possible, then rolled him onto his back and gently but firmly tugged him into the centre.

Fraser placed everyone at a corner of the board. 'On the count of three we'll lift and move John to the stretcher. One, two, three.'

Alison stumbled as she took the weight of her corner. John squealed with agony, and his wife looked ready to cry. 'Oh, John, I'm so sorry. This is awful. I can't do it.'

'You're doing fine,' Fraser placated her. 'Keep coming this way, small, steady steps. That's it. Okay, everyone, put the board on the stretcher.'

Quickly, Nikki attached the straps to keep John stable while Fraser placed the defibrillator at the end of the stretcher. When he began wheeling the stretcher towards the back of the ambulance, Nikki collected up the pack and drugs bag.

'Can I go with John in the ambulance?' Alison asked hesitantly. 'I don't want him to be on his own.'

'Of course you can.' Nikki touched the worried woman lightly on her shoulder. 'You'll have to sit up the front with me so Fraser's got room to move as he keeps monitoring John on the way.'

'Think I'd prefer that. Seeing those machines and cords and things makes me queasy.' Alison climbed aboard and snapped her seat belt in place.

Nikki shut the back doors and squeezed through the middle, pushing past Fraser as she headed for the front. Through gritted teeth she asked, 'Are you ready to go?'

'As John's not critical I'll do another set of obs first.' Fraser glanced at her, a query in his eyes.

'Easier while we're stationary,' Nikki agreed. 'I'll call ED to let them know our ETA and what we've got.'

Waiting for ED to come back to her, she again contemplated Fraser as he worked hard to keep his patient comfortable and his condition from deteriorating. He knew his stuff. He'd have been a brilliant doctor. It came through in everything he did with their patients. He had an almost instinctive feel for their needs, emotionally and physically. He should never have quit his training.

It was blindingly obvious now why he had.

Because of the cancer. But why hadn't he returned to university after his treatment? They'd have given him leave for that, even for a whole year, if he'd wanted it. More questions. Would she ever have all the answers?

Fraser filled the kettle. 'Want a coffee, Nikki?'

No reply.

He glanced around the staffroom and sighed. Not here. Again. Nikki would be upstairs in one of the bedrooms allocated for night crews. Giving him the cold shoulder.

Yep, that's exactly what she was doing, had been doing since he'd been round to her flat to explain and apologise two days ago. Last night and so far tonight all she'd talked to him about had been work and then only when he'd asked her something.

Had he expected anything else? He'd hurt her so much, why should she roll over the moment he explained his actions? She believed he should've told her everything five years ago. He still hadn't told her everything. Hell. He'd been protecting her from having to make impossible decisions. He'd been looking out for himself as well, not wanting her to stay with him out of pity. Not when he'd loved her so much. He'd done a brilliant job of turning her against him, and there was no way of undoing the damage.

What if he told her the rest? Would she go easy on him then?

The kettle clicked off, the small sound loud in the empty room. Reaching for a mug, he shovelled in coffee granules and two spoonfuls of sugar. His sweet tooth had got sweeter over the years.

'Hey, Fraser, make a couple more of those while you're at it, will you?' Chloe bounced into the room, bringing with her a blast of cold outside air. 'It's freezing out there. There'll be ice on the bridges tonight.'

'We've already picked up a woman who skidded near the river.'

Chloe grinned. 'At least our call was an inside job, a wee kiddie having an asthma attack.'

Chloe's crew partner, Ryan, strolled in, rubbing his hands. 'Good, I can smell coffee.' He glanced around. 'Where's Nikki?'

'Upstairs, I guess.' Fraser stirred the drinks ferociously. Last night whenever they hadn't been out in the ambulance Nikki had been holed up in a bedroom, the door firmly shut.

'Again?' Ryan frowned. 'Is she working on her university papers?'

How would he know? 'I didn't know she was studying anything.' Fraser handed around the drinks. He didn't know much at all about Nikki these days. And whose fault was that?

'She's doing a commerce degree.' Ryan flicked the TV on. 'Seems a waste to me when she can make food like this.' He held up a piece of lemon coconut slice he'd taken from a cake tin on the table. Damn it. Fraser punched the switch on the kettle and grabbed another mug. He couldn't stand this silence from her. They owed each other more than that.

Nikki clicked on her email folder. Hopefully there'd be something from her tutor at the extra-mural university regarding her last submission.

Knock, knock. 'Nikki, I've got you a coffee.'

Fraser. Didn't he get it? She didn't want to talk to him.

'Nikki, can I come in?'

No. Go away. Leave me to digest my emotions without taking them out on you. But he wouldn't.

He could be the most stubborn person when he wanted something. Best get it over with. Pushing off the bed, she opened the door wide enough to take the mug Fraser held out to her. 'Thanks.'

He put his foot in the opening. 'Nik, talk to me. Please.'

'Talk to you?' She stared at him. The anger she'd been trying to suppress welled up, making her voice rise, her hand shake so that coffee spilled over her fingers. 'Talk to you. That's rich.'

Fraser stepped forward, effectively forcing her back into the room. As she sat down on the only chair available he closed the door and leaned back against it. 'You're right. I've got a hell of a nerve asking you to share your feelings with me. But we have to get on. It's a bizarre twist of fate that we're both here working side by side, but I'm not leaving. This is what I do, just like you.'

Not what she'd expected. But her anger didn't lessen. 'I'm trying to get my head around it all.'

'I can understand that. It took me weeks.'

'I'm not talking about the cancer, though…' She paused, calmed down a notch, put her mug on the floor. 'That's bad enough. No, what really gets me is that you didn't tell me a thing. Not even when you phoned and told me to call off the wedding. You gave no reason why you didn't want me any more.'

'I always wanted you, Nik.'

'How was I to know that? I'm not psychic.' The words gathered, spewed out. Selfish words coloured with the hurt, bewilderment and humiliation she'd carried for a long time after he'd gone. And she'd thought she'd got past most of this. Who had she been fooling?

'Did it ever occur to you that by telling me about the cancer you'd have saved me years of grief, of wondering if you'd found someone else better-looking, or more exciting in the sack or on your level of intelligence? Did you even have the tiniest clue how I might cope with your shock withdrawal from what I believed to be a mutual relationship?'

Fraser reached for her hand.

She swatted him away, picked up the mug again to wrap her shaking hands around it. Tears streamed down her face. 'The truth would've hurt but at least I'd have known. You made decisions for both of us, and that's the hardest part to understand. Why couldn't you tell me something so important? Not even the possibility of never having children excuses that.'

Fraser crossed to the bed, sat down. Placed a box of tissues beside her. Picked at the cuff of his jersey. Opened his mouth, closed it again.

She watched him closely, trying to read on his face, in his eyes what he obviously couldn't say to her. Then told him, 'I don't know that I'll ever again trust anyone not to do that to me.'

Fraser again reached for her hands, and this time she didn't pull away, hoping the contact would help him tell her what was on his mind.

But he moved his head from side to side. 'I'm just so damned sorry I hurt you. I really am.' He tugged free and stood up. 'I'd better let you get back to whatever you were doing when I barged in.'

Nikki stared at him, disappointment squeezing her. 'You're still doing it. Keeping things from me.' Suddenly she wanted him to know a little more about what she'd been doing in the years they'd been apart. It might help bring them back on an even keel so that at least they could work together smoothly. It might eventually help Fraser talk to her.

'I'm doing a commerce degree. I've got this idea of having my own baking business some time so thought I might as well be prepared for that eventuality.' She gave him a small smile. 'Actually, it's kind of fun, studying. And keeps me off the streets and out of the shops, where I tend to spend too much.'

'I don't remember you being keen on shopping.' He stood near the door, looking genuinely puzzled.

For the first time since he'd arrived back in her life Nikki laughed. 'Oh, boy. You have no idea. Ever since I lost weight I've discovered clothes. And shoes.'

'Guess we didn't have a lot of spare cash when we were living together.'

No, she'd been the breadwinner once she'd completed her chef course. And bread had been about it some days, her wages having been minimal. At least now, since her inheritance from her grandmother, she had more than enough money to indulge her passions. Passions. Cooking still ranked number one, and there was money set aside for the shop she dreamed about.

'So you do want to go back to being a chef one day?'

'When scraping people off roads or picking them up from floors gets too much for me I'll think about it. Some nights after particularly ghastly jobs I want out, but I usually manage to work through that. One day, though, I'll know it's time to move on.' Hesitating, she nibbled her top lip, then dived in. 'Was your decision to quit medicine tied up with having cancer?'

Surprisingly the tension in his shoulders disappeared and he answered easily. 'Yes. Suddenly faced with the knowledge I mightn't live for ever, I couldn't see the point in spending the next years tied down studying.'

She lifted her eyebrows in acknowledgment. 'That's understandable. But going into the ambulance service instead must've been difficult after giving up your ambition. You must think you could do so much more as a doctor.'

'Sometimes.' He looked wistful.

'Did you join immediately after your treatment?'

'No. I went travelling with a couple of mates. Do you remember Kevin and Nigel? They always dropped in as you were making dinner.' When she nodded, he continued, 'The three of us went to Europe, Asia, South America. Had a blast for nearly two years. Worked when the cash ran out, then carried on travelling. I joined the service when I got back to Dunedin. Having done four years' medical study I was fast-tracked through the system and given a permanent job straight away.'

His face was animated, the stress lines ironed out for a few moments. His usually tight mouth lifted in a smile. Those missing years obviously held some great memories for him as well as the bad ones.

'You don't ever think about going back and completing your degree?'

Snap. The smile was gone, the lines were back. 'No.'

Nikki watched Fraser turn and leave the room, his shoulders taut again, his tread heavy on the stairs. Why did she get the impression he was being untruthful?

CHAPTER FIVE

'AHH,' sixty-five-year-old Jeremy Day moaned, kicking out at the bottom of the bed. His elbow connected with Nikki's arm just as she was about to stab his thumb with a sharp.

Ouch. 'Mr Day, please lie still so I can get a drop of blood.' She held back her exasperation, knowing that the man probably couldn't help his attitude right now. A known diabetic, his behaviour suggested his glucose level would be very low, which could be confirmed if they could get a blood sample to test it.

'Hey, Jeremy.' Fraser put a restraining hand on the man's shoulder. 'Take it easy, mate. We're trying to help you.'

The woman in the doorway cried, 'Jeremy, do what they say.'

Nikki asked her, 'How long's your husband been like this?'

'I don't know. He was asleep when I left to

do the shopping at nine this morning. When I got home half an hour ago I found him acting funny.'

A three-hour gap. 'Do you know if he had any breakfast? Or lunch?'

'I left food on the bench but he hasn't touched it.' Mrs Day stared at her husband, despair and love all mixed up on her expression. 'He's so stubborn at times.'

Snap. The sharp pressed into the ball of Jeremy's thumb and a drop of blood oozed out. Nikki quickly used the filter paper to suck up the sample and sighed with relief as she waited for the glucometer to read the blood-sugar level. 'Has this happened before?' she asked Mrs Day.

'Three times. He's not very good about taking his readings. Says if he feels all right then he's fine. The doctor tells him it's very serious not to do everything properly but he won't listen.' Mrs Day looked close to tears.

Beep. The meter showed a glucose reading of two point three. 'Far too low.' Nikki nodded to Fraser, who already had an oral dose of glucose ready.

'Here, Jeremy, let's get this into you then you'll

soon start to feel better.' Fraser held the tiny plastic cup to their patient's lips.

Jeremy jerked his head aside, knocking the liquid down his shirtfront. 'Don't want it.' He rolled onto his side and drew his knees up to his chest.

Calmly, Fraser reached into the medical pack for a second dose. 'Yeah, you do,' he drawled, 'otherwise we take you to hospital for the doctors to sort this out.'

'No. Not going to hospital.'

Nikki sighed. 'We might have to sedate him.'

'Jeremy, here, drink this.' Fraser held the sample cup firmly this time. 'Or we'll put a needle in the back of your hand.'

Slowly, the man opened his eyes and glared at Jeremy. 'I don't want it.'

'I know, but you'll feel so much better when you do. Swallow this then your wife can get you some food.' Fraser pressed the cup gently against Jeremy's lips. 'Please.'

The room was quiet for a moment then Mr Day opened his mouth and Fraser quickly tipped the liquid in.

The tension in Nikki's shoulders relaxed. Very

soon Jeremy would start behaving rationally and they'd be able to discuss what to do next.

'Let's see how you cope walking to the kitchen,' Fraser told the man once he was sitting up and looking more alert.

'I'll be right as rain, you watch.' Jeremy's legs wobbled as he pushed up off the bed but became stronger as he shuffled out of the room.

'Never have figured out that saying,' Fraser muttered he followed their patient, suddenly grabbing the man by his arm. 'Whoops, steady on. You're not in a race, Jeremy.'

'Young man, are you challenging me?' Jeremy looked ten years younger when he smiled.

Nikki grinned. She hadn't found a patient yet that didn't adore Fraser. They were eating out of his hand most of the time, especially once the medication or painkillers started doing their job. He had a way that everyone related to. Even her. No matter how hard she tried to keep him at a distance, he was slowly getting under her skin.

As they drove away Fraser ran his knuckles down his cheek. 'I felt like a bully back there, trying to get Jeremy to take his meds.'

'You? A bully?' Nikki rolled her eyes. 'As if.'

'I was pushing him to do something he didn't want to do.'

'You were saving his life. You were being firm but caring.' He was nothing like his father.

Fraser stopped rubbing his cheek, relaxed back into his seat. 'Thanks for that.'

They made it back to Base and had time to top up glucometer sharps, defib pads and gloves from the store, but not enough to get lunch, before the next call had them scrambling.

'I didn't get to check out that shortbread you brought in,' Fraser groaned.

'Get over it.' She grinned unsympathetically. But when she saw the details of their next call her grin faded. 'Six-year-old girl, unconscious after hitting head on jungle gym at Fairhall School. Charlotte Stevens.' Nikki's stomach plummeted. 'Ella and Mark's little girl. Do you remember them? Ella Wood.'

'I was talking to Mark the other night. Hard to shut him up. Heard everything about Ella and the two kids. Gawd, he's going to be tipped sideways when he hears about this.' Fraser sped through the traffic, the siren blaring. 'Considerate drivers get out of the way,' he roared as he swung wide to avoid a car that had stopped in the middle of the road. 'Ever heard of pulling over?' he yelled.

Thankfully they had a straight run once they left the outskirts of town. As they raced past the vineyards, Nikki filled in a PRF for the child. 'Charlotte Stevens.' Her heart was in her throat. 'I hate going to kids. And this is worse because I know her. She's such a cutie with a mop of curls and a button nose, always talking so fast I can't understand her.'

'Ella and Mark will be glad it's you attending as you know her so well.'

'Talk about pressure.' Nikki nibbled a rough fingernail. 'It freaks me out a bit, hoping I can help them but always wondering if my knowledge is going to be enough. They're so small and I keep thinking about their parents and what I'd say if I couldn't help their baby.'

'You'll be fine. If anyone can save a child it's you,' Fraser commented. 'Seriously, if you ever want a career change, go for emergency nursing. You'd be fantastic.'

'You're kidding? I couldn't do that. I get all

hot and flustered whenever I go to serious emergencies.'

'I'm not aware of that and I work with you. You're known as Miss Cool, Calm and Awesome back at Base.'

She blinked. 'Me? Who said that? I've never heard a thing.' Cool, calm and awesome? Her chest swelled. 'I can live with that.'

Fraser rolled his eyes as he slowed for the school entrance. 'I bet you can.'

They grabbed everything they could possibly need and raced after the teacher, who'd been waiting anxiously for them.

'We haven't moved her at all,' the woman called over her shoulder. 'She fell about twenty minutes ago and still hasn't opened her eyes. Her parents are on their way.'

Nikki swallowed. This didn't sound very good. She glanced across at Fraser as they ran and caught him watching her.

'Miss Cool, Calm and Awesome,' he mouthed as they reached Charlotte.

Blood pooled on the ground beneath Charlotte's head from a large gash above her left temple. Her face appeared whiter than white.

Her little body had twisted as she'd fallen and thankfully no one had tried to straighten her. Who knew what damage could've been inflicted when she hit the concrete?

Nikki looked at Fraser. 'You check her head. I'll take her pulse.' The pulse was impossible to find. Nikki's heart sank as she kept trying to feel the tiniest beat under her fingers. Refusing to give up hope, she was about to ask Fraser if he could try to find it when she felt a ridiculously light movement under her fingertip on the carotid artery. 'Yes,' she muttered, and studied her watch as she began counting. 'Dangerously low,' she muttered a minute later. The blood-pressure reading gave her no more hope.

'Deep compression at the back.' Fraser spoke quietly and with no sense of urgency in his voice, yet she knew he'd be frantic to save this girl.

'We'll load and go. Charlotte needs urgent, expert care. We can't afford to waste time checking her vitals out here.' Basically they'd do all they could to keep her alive while getting her to expert care—fast.

'Definitely. Intubate, collar, transfer to stretcher, and we're gone.'

'If only it was that easy.' Nikki carefully slid the airway tube between Charlotte's teeth and tried to slip it down her throat. Felt relief when the tube finally went into place on the third attempt. Fraser had the oxygen ready. Between them they quickly secured the collar in place. And then Charlotte was carefully shifted onto the stretcher, with as little movement as possible before being transferred to the ambulance.

'Phone her parents, tell them to go to ED immediately,' Nikki told the teacher as she closed the doors. Charlotte would most likely be flown to Wellington for specialist care and Ella and Mark would want to go with her.

'Ready for me to start driving?' asked Fraser.

'Go.' And don't spare the engine, she thought, her heart thumping in trepidation for their tiny patient. The trip took for ever and yet it flew past at a breakneck rate. Seeing the doctors and nurses waiting at the ambulance bay doors was the most welcome sight of her career. Charlotte stood a much better chance now.

After handing over, she turned to Fraser and walked into his arms, laid her cheek against his chest. 'That was scary.'

'But we made a difference. Now it's up to those guys.' His hand stroked her back gently. 'Come on. Let's hope we get back to Base without any further calls. I don't know about you but I could do with a very strong coffee.'

She remained a few more moments in Fraser's arms, trying and failing to wipe out the image of Charlotte's immobile face. She could still feel on her fingertip the child's light pulse. And her heart held anguish for a young girl she adored. Finally, she drew back. 'Very, very strong coffee it is.'

'How do parents cope with something like this?' Fraser said as they drove away. 'When I see accidents like that one I think I'm glad I haven't got kids. I'd be locking them up all the time.'

'To think I wanted to have twelve. I'd have turned grey in no time at all.' Nikki sighed. 'Actually, I only wanted two, a boy and a girl. Funny how things turned out.'

'Nik, you're talking as though it's too late for you to become a mother.'

'It is.' *Because I can't have them with you.*

We're not getting together again. And there isn't anyone else I'd like for the father of my kids.

Pushing into her seat, she stared out the window, not really seeing anything. She'd let her guard down with Fraser for a moment, and look where it had got her. Thinking of unattainable things. Like babies and Fraser all in the same sentence.

At the end of their shift Nikki stretched her back, rolled her shoulders. 'Yee-haa, a day off tomorrow.' Then two nights on. The time was flying past. It was hard to believe Fraser had been here ten days now.

Amber strolled through to the staff lounge, coffee in one hand, a sandwich in the other. 'Are you going shopping tomorrow?'

'As in groceries?' It had been Amber's turn to get those in.

'Done. But there's a sale on at your favourite shoe shop.'

'You're kidding!' Excitement sizzled along Nikki's veins. 'How did I miss that?'

'I'm asking myself the same thing.' Amber grinned. 'They've got the most amazing boots that you're going to want. Black, extra-long to above the knee, with the cutest slender and very high heels.'

'Nikki, you're dribbling,' Fraser called from the doorway. His eyes looked slightly misty. Did boots turn him on? So what if they did?

Nikki grinned despite her tummy suddenly tightening. 'What would a guy know about these things?'

But as Fraser's eyes turned a roasted-coffee-bean colour she decided this guy knew quite a lot, even if only how boots looked on tall, slim women. Her bubble burst. She was of average height and definitely not slim so his fantasy, if that's what it was, wasn't about her.

'Guess you'll be up early to fit your run in before the shoe shop opens.' Amber bumped the table with her hip, splashed coffee over her forest-green uniform jersey. 'Great.' As she wiped at the spill she asked, 'Did you two have a quiet day?'

Nikki shook her head. 'Nope. We hardly stopped.' After Charlotte they'd been up the Awatere Valley for a broken femur and torn artery, followed by a car versus tree that had involved a family of four and required two ambulances. 'Any news on Charlotte?' she asked the room in general.

Gavin looked up from the newspaper. 'The little girl flown to Wellington? Not a word so far.'

Fraser still waited at the door, his day pack slung over his shoulder, his gaze on her. 'Can we phone anyone?'

'I don't want to bother Mark and Ella's families. I'll check with ED later to see if they've heard anything.'

'Come on, let's get out of here. We're already an hour past sign-off time.' Fraser jerked a thumb over his shoulder. 'We could join Mike and the others for a beer at the pub. Wind down a bit before going home.' His voice was soft, quiet, as though afraid of frightening her off the idea.

'Sounds like a plan.' Shrugging into her jacket, she saw Amber watching her with a knowing smirk on her face. 'What?'

'Nothing.' Her friend grinned.

'Good.' Checking Fraser wasn't within hearing, she added, 'Drop it, Amber. We barely speak in the truck, so we're not going to have a rave at the pub.'

'Where's your SUV?' Fraser asked as he closed the outside door behind them.

'Along Scott Street a bit, under that old oak.'

'I'll walk with you. Mine's a bit farther on.' Then he asked, 'Why an SUV? Why not a zippy little car?'

'My brothers.'

'Pardon?'

'All part of the making sure Nikki is safe programme.' Which was all well and good at times. 'But I didn't argue too much as I do like my vehicle. It's cool.' Hurrying along the footpath, Nikki tugged the zip of her jacket higher. 'Dang, but it's cold out here.'

'You've got a flat.' Fraser stepped off the pavement and bent down on the far side of her four-wheel-drive vehicle. 'I'll change it for you.'

'No need. I can manage.' Not that it would be fun in the dark and the light drizzle that had just begun.

'Nikki, I'm not walking away and leaving you to change a tyre. Got a torch?'

'Yep.' Waving her electronic key, she popped the locks, found the torch and opened the back door to retrieve the wheel brace and jack. 'You're not taking the slightest bit of notice of me, just like my brothers.' Fraser being the forceful, caring male wasn't the Fraser she wanted to remember. Too close to home.

He brushed past her. 'I'll get the spare wheel out.' His shoulder sliding against hers should've been innocuous. It wasn't. She felt as though she'd been zapped with a high-voltage electric shock.

Leaping back, she dropped the brace. As she bent to pick it up her head bumped Fraser's thigh. Talk about turning everything into a circus. 'Sorry,' she muttered.

Fraser's hand gripped her shoulder, tugged her close. In the gloom he peered into her face. 'Hey, Nik, take it easy. We're changing a tyre here, nothing more exciting than that.'

That was the problem. She didn't want anything more exciting either, but after days spent driving around Blenheim with him beside her, or sitting in the common room at the station talking cases, her hormones seemed to have a different opinion from the sane side of her brain. Shocked, she stood staring at the back of his head as he wrestled with undoing the wheel nuts, willing the goose-bumps lifting her skin to lie down.

'Hold the torch so I can see.' Fraser handed her the nuts and hunkered down again, his big hands making easy work of removing the offending tyre.

Her tongue cleaved to the roof of her suddenly dry mouth as a vivid memory came to mind of those hands, those fingers making easy work of bringing her alive as she and Fraser had rolled around their bed in the flat. Why now, after an awful day, did she have to recall that particular picture?

Slumping against the side of the vehicle, she struggled to keep the torch pointed exactly where Fraser wanted it. The beam shook. Her head buzzed and her tummy tightened with unbelievable longing.

'Now for that beer.' Fraser clipped the old tyre into place in the back of Nikki's vehicle and slammed the door shut. He turned and bumped up against Nik. Why hadn't that peony scent warned him how close she was?

He had to touch her, hold her. Like he had earlier outside the ED. Nothing like that. That had been platonic, or as near platonic he was capable of being with Nikki. Which was diddly squat. But right now he wanted—no, needed—to wrap his arms around her and hold her tight, feel her chest rising and falling, her hands on his back, her fingers pressing firmly. He ached with the need. She stood so close he could feel her sharp, quick breaths on his chin.

An urge to kiss her gripped him, too strong to be denied. Placing his arms around her waist, he gently drew her nearer, afraid that at any moment she'd slap him away. At last his lips covered her sweet mouth. His tongue slid slowly inside, tasting her, stirring up so many wonderful, warm feelings and memories from the past.

Nikki didn't pull away. Instead, she leaned into him, a soft groan slipping over her bottom lip. One hand clasped the back of his neck. To prevent him getting away? She needn't worry. He wasn't going anywhere. His legs didn't have the strength required to walk.

He deepened his kiss, sliding his tongue farther into that warm mouth, exploring her sweetness, her heat. Sending his hormones into overdrive. When his arms tightened further Nikki's breasts pressed hard against his chest. Even through the thick layers of uniform they both wore he was aware of her shape, her heat, her body.

'I want you.'

Fraser blinked. Had he just said that? Then why wasn't Nikki leaping out of his arms and locking herself inside the SUV?

'No,' Nikki growled against his mouth. But didn't pull away.

Nikki had heard him. The words had been real, hadn't been in his head. He wanted, needed her. But this was Nikki, the woman who'd been avoiding him for days other than to discuss emergency procedures. She was kissing him back. The woman he should be staying well clear of—for her sake. He knew he had to step away from her. But she tasted so good, how could he let go of her? Twisting his head for better access to her mouth, his hands on her chin, thumbs rubbing lightly, the world shrank to this spot. No one, nothing else mattered.

The drizzle turned into a downpour.

They sprang apart. Nikki leapt for her SUV.

'See you at the pub,' Fraser yelled as he

slammed her door shut and raced for his vehicle ten metres farther down the road.

Inside his home-built truck he slumped over the steering-wheel, banging his head with his fist. What an idiot he was. Nikki wouldn't be at the pub when he got there. Not after he'd lost his cool and kissed her. She might've been kissing him back but he'd bet his best cricket bat she was already regretting it. She'd be berating herself for giving in so easily when she'd spent every day they'd worked together making absolutely sure that he understood there was nothing between them any more.

Reaching for the ignition, he sighed. Might as well have a beer anyway. He needed it now, even if Nikki didn't.

'Wakey-wakey, sleepyhead.' Amy's voice crawled into Nikki's head, dragging her into the morning.

Rolling onto her back, Nikki groaned as pain slammed into her eyeballs and threatened to blow the top off her head. 'Ahh, what happened?' She squeezed her eyes tight.

Amber tugged the curtains wide open. 'I'd say you drank too much at the pub last night.'

That could explain the bongo drums in her head. That probably had as much to do with her state as the three vodkas. Nothing to do with the fact she'd lain awake for hours dissecting that bone-crunching, mind-shattering kiss after all. 'I didn't eat much yesterday because we were so busy.' Nikki partially opened one eye. 'Shut those curtains, will you? The light's hurting me.'

Amber sounded disgustingly cheerful. 'So nothing to do with kissing Fraser?'

'How do you know that?' The drums picked up their pace. So it hadn't been a bad dream. It had been real. And it hadn't been bad either.

Amber plonked down on the end of the bed, tucking one foot under her bottom. 'Gavin and I drove past on our way to a call.'

Nikki swallowed hard. 'Do me a favour and keep that to yourself. It won't be happening again.' What had she done? Kissing Fraser was worse than running stark naked down Market Street on a busy Friday night.

Tugging her pillow from under her head, Nikki pulled it over her face. She couldn't bear to think about last night. Whatever had possessed her to return Fraser's kiss instead of pushing him away? It would be so humiliating when she next saw him. He'd think she was an easy touch. That she'd enjoyed kissing him and had wanted more was completely irrelevant. They weren't getting back together.

'Nikki.' Amber leaned forward to stab her shoulder with a finger. 'Come on. You've got to get up.'

'Go away,' she muttered into the pillow as tears began squeezing out her scrunched-shut eyes. 'I can't believe I did that.'

'Want a coffee?'

Nikki eased the pillow aside and glared at her friend. 'Leave me to sleep for the next ten years, will you?' Hopefully by then Fraser would have left town again and she'd be able to step outside her front door.

'Can't do that. Your brother's coming around any minute.'

'Which one?' Her stomach rolled unpleasantly.

'Jay.'

Nikki stared at Amber, trying to see her properly through the fog in her eyes. 'There's a hint of red in your cheeks when you say Jay's name.'

'I've just had a hot shower.' Amber looked away, fiddling with the bedspread.

'You've got the hots for my brother.' Nikki's head pounded harder. She needed to warn Amber about Jay. Another time, she decided on a tender breath.

'Lover boy's here.'

'What?' Nikki's skull split wide as she screeched, 'Who do you mean?' But she knew. Fraser had turned up. Why?

'He brought your car round.' When Nikki squinted at her, Amber added, 'Apparently you were adamant you weren't driving last night.'

Nikki flipped her hand left, right. 'I'd never risk it. I've seen too many alcohol-induced road smashes.' She shut her eyes again. 'Tell him thanks and I'll see him at work.'

'No can do. He's sitting in the kitchen with take-out coffees for us all. Says he's not leaving until he's seen you.' Amber stood up, a sly smile on her face. 'I suspect he'll come in here if you don't make an appearance soon. He's that determined. You've made a hit, Nikki.'

You have no idea what I've done. None whatsoever. Another thought crashed into her skull. 'Jay's coming around.'

'So?'

'Ever seen a match thrown into a drum of petrol?' Jay was the most protective in a bevy of protective brothers. She could almost feel sorry for Fraser, except he was big enough to fight his own battles.

Fraser paced the length of the tiny kitchen. Five steps to the wall with a shoebox-sized window that looked out onto the damp concrete square that served as the back yard. A washing line was strung from one side to the other, with underwear hanging from it. Gulp. Nikki's?

In an effort to blank that sight from his head he turned, took five steps back to the door leading into the hall. This tiny flat had surprised him. He'd expected something roomier, sunnier, like the enormous, rambling homestead Nikki had grown up in.

Reaching the door, he heard the girls murmuring in one of the rooms off the short hall. He turned back to the window. Would Nikki make an appearance? If she refused to come out of her room he'd go to see her. He had to make sure she understood last night had been a one-off. His fingertips tingled, vividly reminding him of her satin skin as he'd caressed her neck, her cheeks. Unfortunately. He stopped. Stared around. Unfortunately? Since when did he want to get back with Nik?

Only since you left her five years ago.

His head spun. Really?

The back door burst open, letting in a draught of icy air—and one of four men Fraser definitely did not want to come face to face with yet.

'McCall, what the hell are you doing in my sister's flat?'

'Waiting to see Nikki.' Fraser stood straighter, taller. At six-one he mightn't quite measure up to Jay's height but he was damned if he was going to let that bother him. He would not be intimidated by the Page brothers. He needed them back on side, like they used to be before the wedding debacle, which meant proving he was looking out for their sister and in no way upsetting her.

Which meant explaining and apologising for

the past. By the angry gleam in Jay's eyes it was obvious Nikki hadn't said a word about the cancer. Which was good. It was up to him. He didn't believe for a minute that the Page family would immediately forgive him but hopefully none of them would want to beat the crap out of him either.

'She won't see you.'

He was probably right. 'You know we work together—'

'Hey, Jay.' Nikki slunk into the cramped kitchen, Amber following.

Nik looked tired and dishevelled; that gorgeous mane of dark blonde hair free of its usual constraints and falling haphazardly over her shoulders. She wound her arms around her brother and gave him a brief peck on his cheek.

If only she'd do the same to me, Fraser thought. 'Hi, Nikki,' he croaked, his tongue so thick it filled his mouth. He'd give a year's pay to run his hands through her hair, to feel its softness sliding across his skin. Her classy, satin dressing gown outlined her fabulous bottom perfectly and switched on his desire. Just like that. Bad timing. If he stood absolutely still, maybe no one would notice his reaction to the goddess standing before him.

'Fraser.' Nikki barely acknowledged him.

So he was back out in the cold. Two steps forward, three back today.

Jay kept a protective arm around her waist as he asked, 'What's McCall doing here?'

Nikki blinked, nodded perfunctorily. 'Fraser brought my vehicle home. Everyone from work went to the pub and I didn't want to drive afterwards.'

Jay grunted, relaxed a tad. 'Oh, thanks, McCall.'

'Yeah, thanks.' Nikki picked up a coffee. 'This for me?'

'Yes. It's probably gone cold by now.'

'Thanks anyway.' She sipped cautiously, before pouring the coffee down her throat. Next she opened a cupboard, removed a pan and placed it on the stove. From the fridge she removed a carton of eggs and a bottle of cream, moving carefully as though she hurt. 'Breakfast, anybody?'

'Count me in,' Amber looked at Jay, hope in her eyes. 'You staying?'

'If Nikki's cooking, I am.' Jay squashed himself down at the tiny table and folded his long legs under the chair.

Crack. Crack. Crack. Slowly the pan filled with eggs.

Amber asked Fraser, 'Do you need a ride somewhere after breakfast?'

He hadn't said he was staying. 'I'll walk home.' A five-kilometre hike would be good for what ailed him. He should have put his running gear on.

Nikki turned, fixed him with those azure eyes that had haunted his sleep last night. 'I'll drop you back.' The whisk in her hand dripped egg on the floor.

Fraser gave her a tentative smile. 'Thanks, but you're cooking breakfast. Besides, you're not dressed for going outside.' He reached around her for the dishcloth, bent down to wipe up the mess.

'You can stay for some food,' Jay drawled, his gaze crossing from his sister to Fraser and back, a distinct question in his eyes. 'Got enough eggs in that pan, Nikki?'

Why was Jay suddenly okay with him being there? Had Nikki told him about the cancer after all? Fraser hoped his old mate wasn't feeling sorry for him. That was the last thing he wanted. But he was getting an opportunity to be on speaking terms with his old friend. 'I'll stay.'

'I've got more than enough.' Nikki glanced at Jay then back to him before slowly turning back to the pan and whisking cream into the eggs. When she added chopped fresh herbs to the pan his mouth watered. He remembered this process. Nik made the most delicious scrambled eggs ever. Then he saw the whisk slow and stop as Nikki stared out the window. Seeing what? Thinking what? About them? Last night?

Behind him Jay asked, 'Are you back permanently, McCall?'

Dragging his gaze away from Nikki, he faced her brother. 'Yes.'

Jay studied him with a worrying intensity. His gaze shifted to his sister for a moment before returning to bore into Fraser. A warning?

He hurried to explain. 'Dad's got dementia and Mum needs me here. Besides, Blenheim's home and that's where I want to be these days.'

Nikki's head had lifted, tilted slightly to one side. Listening carefully.

So he added, 'I also want to qualify as an AP while Dad's capable of understanding. It's something I owe him.' It would never make up for the medical degree he'd dropped out of, but at least he'd have finished something for once in a long time.

Suddenly a similar smell to burning paella teased his nostrils. 'The eggs are burning.'

Nikki spun around and snatched up the pan. 'I never burn eggs. I'm a good cook.'

He was almost relieved. Now he could get away from the daunting questions in Jay's eyes. He'd tell Jay what had happened to him, but he intended telling all Nikki's family, just not one person at a time. 'Guess that's breakfast, then. I'll head home now.'

The pan clattered into the sink and the sound of vigorous scraping filled the room. 'I should never have started to cook this morning. Too many distractions,' Nikki muttered, loud enough for only him to hear.

Jay spoke over the noise. 'I'll give you a lift, McCall.'

Nikki paled, and the pot scrub in her hand

came close to snapping. 'No, it's all right. I'll get dressed and take him.'

'Sis, I've got to go to the pharmacy and pick up some drugs I've ordered for a dog anyway. It's no problem to take Fraser with me. Right, McCall?'

What could he say? *No, I'd rather crawl all the way?* 'Thanks.' He wanted his old life back, right? And that meant playing sport with the local teams, going to the pub with old mates. He couldn't win Nikki's heart back, but if he mended some bridges with old mates, especially Jay, he could settle down here where his roots were.

CHAPTER SIX

NIKKI rushed into the farmhouse kitchen, tugging her jacket off and tossing it on a hook by the door. The scent of fresh rosemary from the roast lamb wafted tantalisingly around the kitchen. 'Sorry I'm late, Mum. Amber and I went shopping. I also got highlights put through my hair and had my nails done. Time got away from me.' Glancing down at her new ankle boots, Nikki grinned. They were so cool. 'Plus the torrential rain forced me to drive slowly.'

'Never mind, I'm just glad you made it.' Her mother, Rose, smiled as she handed Nikki a wooden spoon. 'Just in time to make the gravy.'

'No problem.'

Just then a shout of familiar laughter snatched her attention, wiped her smile away. 'Fraser?' She turned to stare into the games room off the side of the kitchen, where three of her brothers stood shoulder to shoulder at the pool table.

Fraser was lining up a shot. Beau and Jay were heckling him. 'He's here? With the boys?' Her voice lifted in a shrill squeak. They seemed almost relaxed with him, not trussing him up like a chicken so they could take turns hurting him. 'But—?'

'Jay invited him to stay for dinner.' Rose stood beside her, looking in the same direction. 'It's a bit like old times.'

No. Nothing like that at all. Old times meant everyone got on, meant she and Fraser were in love, meant they had a joint future ahead of them. She'd been so happy then. There was no going back now. Worse, her family were supposed to support her, not let Fraser back in. Despair shook her. 'Thanks a lot, everybody,' she muttered.

'Took some guts, walking in here, I'll give him that,' Nikki's dad muttered as he carved the enormous leg of lamb on the meat platter. 'He told us he'd talked to you the other night, and then he apologised for his behaviour the day of your wedding.'

Wow. Fraser really did mean to clear up everything that had gone wrong. Nikki nodded, her gaze still fixed on him. 'Did he just turn up out of the blue? Were all the boys here?'

'Yep, about an hour ago when everyone but you and Jordan had arrived. Had a couple of six packs with him. Told us about the cancer, too.' Her dad continued carving. 'He filled Jordan in on the facts when he turned up.'

Nikki shook her head slowly. 'How did the boys take Fraser's story? Is he back in favour now?' Had her brothers all accepted the situation and put the past behind them as easily as that? This was her territory. Those big men in the games room with Fraser were her over-protective siblings. Where did this leave her? Was she wrong to hold out on him?

Pulling her gaze away, she concentrated on heating the basting juices from the lamb, slowly adding seasonings until she was happy with the flavour.

Her dad watched her, love for her in his eyes. 'I know it still doesn't make it right how he treated you, but I guess we've got to cut him some slack. Fraser was a part of this family until then.'

Nikki swallowed. There had been moments over the past few days when she'd thought the same thing, but then she'd think that if he'd really and truly loved her, she'd have been the first person he'd have told. 'Yeah, well, that's why he should've felt comfortable talking to us.'

Stirring the gravy, letting it thicken slowly, she glanced over at the man who had kissed her a few days ago. A short kiss as far as kisses went, but potent. Fraser's lips on hers had reminded her of some of the good times they'd had. Memories she wasn't sure she needed now, because they gave her hope. Hope for something she wasn't anywhere near ready to think about. Or was even sure she wanted to follow up on.

Her dad tapped the carving knife on the edge of the plate. 'Fraser's got a good heart, lass. He's come home to help his mother take care of Ken. Which—' her dad carved another slice of meat '—considering how Ken used to treat Fraser, is nothing short of a miracle.'

'You mean because Ken bullied Fraser?' Fraser had told her about being taunted by his father if he ever failed a school test or didn't score enough runs in a cricket match. Not meeting his father's demanding expectations had made Fraser's childhood harsh. 'I guess that shows Fraser's good nature.' Dang.

'It does.' Her dad sighed sadly. 'I always figured your man over there left town the very day he finished school to get away from his old man. The rumours were rife when he was young. I remember finding him in the implement shed here one day, sobbing because he'd missed out on the maths prize and his father would be angry. He was seven, for pity's sake.'

'He's not my man.' Her response was automatic, but also the truth. It didn't matter why they'd broken up, but they had, and that was that. But what her dad had said was true. Fraser hadn't said much but she'd seen the hurt in his eyes whenever he'd mentioned his father.

Fraser straightened and challenged Jay with a long drink from his bottle of beer. Bloke speak. Then he glanced sideways and locked eyes with her. The air leaked from her lungs. Fraser. He'd been badly hurt, as badly as she had, if not worse, by his illness and who knew what else. Caution hovered in the back of his eyes, as if half expecting someone or something to snatch away his happiness. In the past she'd have said,

'Serves him right', but now she only wanted to hug him and take away that wariness, to assure him everything was all right. Which was strange. She wanted to hug Fraser? As in comfort him? She shook her head. Weird.

Her mother tapped her shoulder. 'Mind that gravy, love.'

Too late. 'It's split.' Heck, take her mind off the pan for one moment and look what happened. Fraser happened, that's what. Once again, she'd made a basic cooking error because he'd distracted her. At this rate she'd have to give up cooking.

'Not much you can do with that now. We'll have to go without.' Nikki's mother handed her a plate laden with roasted vegetables. 'Put that on the table, will you? And relax. Fraser's not going to hurt you tonight or any other night.'

Nikki turned back to her parents. 'You're both so sure. He's apologised and suddenly the front door's open again.' The plate was heavy and she gripped the edges.

Her mum leaned closer. 'Come on, my girl. He's faced up to a family he knows he treated badly. And he's done it with good grace, honestly and openly. Everyone's entitled to a second chance at least once in their life.'

'Hey, Nikki. Bet you weren't expecting to see me before Tuesday.' Fraser had appeared in front of her. He leaned close, asked quietly, 'Are you okay with me being here? Because I can go if you'd prefer it.'

A second chance, her mother had said. What did that mean? Give Fraser another chance with her? Or the opportunity to be a part of her family again? To play sport with Jay and his mates? To turn up to join in whatever was happening here? Like tonight?

The heavy platter tilted precariously in her hands. Reluctantly, she looked into his eyes, saw nothing but honesty. Which made it hard to tell him to go. With a hesitant smile she held the dish out. 'Put that on the table, will you?'

'I take it I'm staying.'

'You should.' Amazing, but she meant it. Must be something in the air.

Glancing in the direction of the dining room, Nikki noticed her two sisters-in-law watching them, nothing but genuine concern for her in their eyes. Or was it for Fraser? Turning back to him, she asked, 'How hard was it to walk in here after all this time?'

'A little easier than rifles at sunset would've been.' Fraser smiled that delicious smile that had always got to her, making her putty in his hands. And now made her think he did deserve a second chance. Oh, boy. As she blinked, Fraser continued, 'I'm a useless shot.'

She smiled tentatively, suddenly wanting to move forward, step over the past lying between them. 'Then I'm glad it didn't come to that.'

'Come on, you two. We're starving in here,' Beau called out.

'And that food's getting cold, Fraser.' Jordan, brother number two, added his bit. 'Talking of cold, I'll throw another chunk of wood on the fire. That rain hasn't eased off all day and the temperature's dropped further.'

'The river was higher than I've seen it in years when I came out,' Nikki said, suddenly glad to get back to talking about ordinary, everyday things. 'So much for spring pushing winter out of the way. Just hope there haven't been too many lambs born yet.'

'There've been a few out this way recently.'

Jay looked around the many dishes on the table. 'Where's the gravy?'

'I wrecked it.'

Jay grinned. 'First burnt eggs last week and now ruined gravy. You need cooking lessons, sis.'

'Still giving you a hard time.' Amusement glinted at her from Fraser's eyes.

'Brothers can be such a pain at times.' Nikki grinned and relaxed completely for the first time all evening. 'But Beau's going to have to start behaving sensibly soon. He and Yvonne are pregnant.'

Fraser reached a hand out. 'Congratulations, Beau, Yvonne. That's fantastic news.'

'Auntie Nikki has already drawn up a babysitting roster so that she gets more turns than anyone else.' Yvonne grinned and gave Beau a peck on his bristly cheek. 'But she'll have to wait a few years until we're in need of a break. I can't imagine ever wanting to let someone else look after my baby.'

Rose smiled knowingly. 'You'll be glad of a night out with Beau after sleepless nights and full-on days, believe me.'

Fraser winked at Nikki. 'Auntie Nikki, eh?'

'Just wish the rest of them would get on with producing heirs for me to play with.' And fill the gap in her heart that should've been filled by her own children.

There were only two vacant seats at the table, side by side, apart from those her parents always sat in. A manipulation by her family? Or coincidence? She'd go for the latter, and try not to question what those big oafs who claimed to care so much about her were up to. Or were they silently telling her to take another look at Fraser? That they'd vetted him and found him good enough for their sister after all? Totally confused, Nikki sat down and deliberately immersed herself in the light banter flowing around and over the table. This was how families behaved. At least, hers did, and always had.

As the meal progressed Nikki became increasingly aware of the man sitting beside her. It seemed that every time she moved she brushed against him. 'Salt, please.' And her thigh touched his as she reached to take the shaker. 'Peas, ta.' Her arm moved over Fraser's. Her elbow nudged him as she cut her meat. When she tapped her foot in exasperation, her toes tapped the top of his foot.

This was far worse than being shut in an ambulance with him all day. And that was bad enough.

'How are you finding being back in Blenheim?' her father asked Fraser when he could get a word in around his sons' banter—about halfway through dessert.

'At first everything seemed exactly the same as the day I left for university. But Blenheim has changed, Allan. More people live here, the vineyards have spread farther out from the town, and now it's the people I grew up with who are working on the land, running the businesses. I'm very glad to be back.'

Out in the hall the phone rang and Jay pushed his chair back. 'I'll get that. Might be someone remembering it's my birthday.'

'How could anyone forget when he told the whole town?' Beau grinned.

Jay was back, his face bleak. 'That was the police. The bridge is out. The river's burst its banks. Our four-wheel-drive tractor's needed up by the bend to pull a campervan out from where it crashed over the railing into the water.'

'Sounds dangerous, son.'

'It gets worse. Two people are trapped inside. Nikki, Fraser, I took the liberty of saying you were here and the SARS co-ordinator wants you to attend. There could be injuries.'

'Not a problem. I'll change into workboots.' Nikki stood up. 'Jay's in the search-and-rescue team these days,' she informed Fraser while mentally running through what might be available in the house to take to the scene in case of injuries. 'Mum, I'll take your first-aid kit and some blankets.'

Fraser pushed his chair back. 'Has the ambulance been called?'

Jay answered over his shoulder as he headed for the back door. 'Yes, but they're going the long way. There's another breach of the river bank closer to town that's causing chaos.'

Nearly an hour would be added to the crew's trip, then. 'Guess it really is up to us.' Nikki grimaced.

Beau was already at the door. 'I'm coming, too. Might be something I can do to help.' Within moments three brothers were kitted out in wet-weather gear and stomping through the rain to one of the large four-wheel-drive vehicles parked by the shed, while Jay headed to the shed and the tractor. Allan called to Fraser, 'Keep an eye on my girl, will you? I know what she's like when she thinks someone needs her help.'

'I'll be glued to her at the hip.' Fraser took the pile of blankets Nikki's mother handed him and stuffed them into plastic bin liners for protection from the rain. He nodded at Nikki. 'We'll take your SUV. My little heap will sink in the first puddle we come to.'

'Glued to me at the hip?'

'Where you go, I go.' He grinned that wicked grin of his that turned her toes upwards, fizzed her blood.

Thank goodness it would be chilly out in the rain.

Fraser drove, following the guys down the long drive and out onto the sodden road, surprised that Nikki had tossed him the keys. Normally she would be proving that she was as good as any of her brothers.

Slap, slap went the wipers. *Whack, whack* went

his brain. He'd gone out to her family home that afternoon, not really knowing how well he'd be accepted by Nikki's family despite Jay's genuine invitation after he'd heard his story. No one had mentioned the past, which had perversely put him on edge, tightening his gut, tensing his shoulders.

They'd just waited for him to say his piece, which had been hard to do with those men all lined up, hands on hips, waiting. Everybody but everybody knew you didn't fool around with Nikki or else those brothers would be down on you like a load of hay bales. But Jay had stood beside him.

Parking on the edge of the hard by the group of people clad in waterproof gear peering over the edge into the raging waters of the usually quiet Wairau River, Fraser commented, 'Those spotlights on that farm truck give the whole place an eerie look.'

'There's the campervan.' Nikki pointed to the van bobbing precariously in the river, water lapping at the bottom of the windows. 'Those poor people must be terrified.' She jumped out of the vehicle and stomped through the puddles to join her brothers.

Fraser followed, pausing at the river's edge, the sight making him whistle through his teeth. 'Hell, those folks are lucky not to have been swept away.'

'The current could still roll the van at any moment.' Beau appeared at his elbow.

Jay joined them. 'It's going to be a job and a half getting those people out of there. I doubt I can pull the camper back onto land. It's too far over the edge and I'll be pulling against the current. A crane might do the trick tomorrow. In the meantime, I can anchor the van while the guys evacuate those people.'

Nikki stood on Jay's other side. 'If that was me stuck in there, I'd be screaming in fear.'

Fraser grimaced. If it had been Nikki in that van *he'd* be screaming with fear. And there'd be no stopping him moving mountains to get her out. 'Do we know exactly who's inside the camper?' he asked Jay.

'A woman and a teenager. They'd been parked on the river bank most of the afternoon but must've decided it was time to move away from the river. Pity they didn't make that decision hours ago.' Jay stomped off to his tractor.

Fraser turned to Nikki. 'Why don't you wait in your vehicle until we're wanted? No point in getting soaked unnecessarily.'

'Because then I wouldn't know what's going on.' She glared at him. 'As soon as Jay's secured the van I'm going to see if I can reach those people. There's a strong possibility one or both were injured when they tipped over the edge. Either of them could've slammed headfirst into the windscreen or dash.'

Fraser's blood chilled, slowed. 'You are not going anywhere near that vehicle. Or the bank.'

Beau stepped in front of her. 'No, Nikki. I don't think so. What if the bank gives out completely and the van gets washed away?'

'You could be hurt. Drowned.' Fraser added his fears.

Jay had spun around and stomped straight back to Nikki. 'Where did you get that dumb idea from, sis? You are not going near that river.' Even in the dim light his fear for his sister was easy to see. 'You think we haven't got enough to deal with without you getting into trouble? Try climbing down to the front of that van in this rain and see what happens. You'll slip for sure. Stay with Fraser and Beau until we can bring those people to you.'

Nikki laid a hand on Jay's arm. 'It's okay, I'll be careful.'

Jay shrugged her hand away. 'You're not going there.'

'You could tie a rope around my waist.' Defiance tightened her voice and stabbed Fraser in the gut.

'No way,' he all but shouted, and was rewarded with rolling eyes and a tight mouth.

'You think we're not going to do everything we can to get those two out of there?' Jay snapped. 'We've got specially trained people to do this.'

'None of your lot can do more than basic first aid. I can.' Nikki glared at her brother. 'I understand why you're worried but this is different. I can look after myself, Jay. And your guys will make sure nothing happens to me.'

Jay grunted. 'You want me scared witless?'

'No, I don't.' Some eye contact went down between Nikki and her brother before she turned her fiery glare on Fraser. 'Our job is to help people.'

Fraser responded quickly. 'No, Nik. It's the job of the SAR's guys to get them out of there. Then you can do your magic medical stuff.'

Jay prodded Nikki's shoulder. 'Seriously, sis, I want you safe on firm ground, not giving me a heart attack while you're hanging over that wild river in a vehicle that's relying on a rope to keep it out of trouble.' He raced towards his tractor.

Just then shouts came from below them. 'Help me. Mum's not waking up.' The young voice from the camper's now open skylight was filled with terror.

'That does it. I can get in through that skylight.' Nikki charged after Jay, calling, 'Hurry up with securing that van. I'm going in.' She approached the other men and whatever she said quickly had them fixing her into a harness attached to a long safety rope on pulleys.

Fraser's heartbeat was all over the place. She couldn't go out there. What if she slipped? He stepped forward. 'I'll go.'

'Like you're going to fit those shoulders through that gap.' Her eyes glittered at him then suddenly softened. 'Can you get the first-aid stuff that I brought from home?'

He wanted to tie her to her SUV so she couldn't do such a damned-fool thing, not be aiding her in this crazy scheme. But she wasn't about to listen to him.

'Okay,' he acquiesced, but it should be him going. He wanted to help those people as much as she did, and at least then she'd be safe.

'Fraser,' she said softly, 'I'll be fine. These guys will make sure of that.'

And I'll be terrified every single second until you're back on firm ground. 'You're right.' He strove for a normal voice, speaking around a huge blockage in his throat. Nikki needed him focused on the job. 'I wish we had the ambulance and all its gear.'

Her hand was shaking when he handed her the bag of supplies. He changed tack. She needed support, not argument. 'You can do this, Nik. You'll be just fine.'

Please, his heart begged. *Please don't slip, fall, hurt yourself. Please put your safety first*, but he knew that was a hopeless request so he kept it to himself and stood with Beau, watching while his heart thumped continuously.

The SAR men wouldn't let Nikki go until Jay had the wire cable secured from his tractor to the camper and one of them had gone over to perch on the van's roof first. The moment they gave her the nod she was moving down the bank as fast as possible, crossing the raging water. Using the spare wheel attached to the back of the van, she began hauling herself up. She slipped, grasped the wheel and hung for a moment, her feet kicking at the water. The rope did its job, holding her safe, although at an awkward angle.

'Hell.' Fraser stood on the edge of the bank, mindless of his own safety, holding his breath. Even knowing about the safety rope, his mind tossed up pictures of Nikki being washed away, rolling and bouncing down the river. Then she began hauling herself upwards again. Slowly, one hand grip at a time. He'd give anything to swap places with her.

'Damn it, Nikki. Be careful,' Beau muttered beside him. 'Why couldn't she wait until the guys brought those people to her?'

'Because she cares too much,' Fraser admitted. 'Hell, I want to go and help them, so why wouldn't Nik?'

'You ambos are all the same, needing to make everyone better.'

'Yeah, and you're not? Coming out in these conditions to rescue these people?' Fraser nudged Beau in the arm. 'Eh, Dr Page?'

'A lot of use being a gynaecologist is,' Beau retorted before calling to Jay, 'How are your lot going to get everyone off that campervan?'

'The same way Nikki and Andy went on board. Ropes and pulleys.'

It took for ever to evacuate the boy, Bryne, who'd had his left arm strapped across his chest by Nikki. When he was on firm ground Fraser led him to the SUV and settled him on the back seat. 'Let's take a look at that arm.'

'The lady said it's broken,' Bryne told him. 'Here.' He tapped his lower arm.

Beau joined them. 'Did Nikki give you anything for the pain?'

Bryne shook his head. 'Do you think Mum's going to be all right? She's unconscious and her head's bleeding.'

'I'm sure she'll be good to go as soon as we

get her to hospital. What did she bang her head on?' Fraser asked.

'I don't know. I was in the back when we went over the bank. It was scary. I thought I was going to die.'

'Hey.' Fraser lightly tapped Bryne's hand. 'You're safe now, okay? Think of the story you can tell your mates.'

Nikki poked her head in the door. 'How are you doing, Bryne? Mum's safe now. My brother, Beau, he's a doctor and he'll see to your mum.'

Fraser couldn't help himself. He reached for Nikki, ran a finger down her frozen cheek. 'Glad you're back,' he whispered.

'So am I. It was darned freaky out there.'

It had been darned freaky here, too.

Flashing lights announced the arrival of the ambulance. 'Here comes the cavalry.' It was easier to focus on that than think about the danger Nikki had put herself in. She was safe and that should be all that mattered. The fact that his heart was still knocking hard against his ribs was irrelevant. Wasn't it?

Nikki called through the rain still pouring relentlessly out of the sky, 'Hey, guys, typical. Wait till the hard work's done before turning up.'

'I think we've been to Christchurch and back, trying to find a way through,' Mike said as he and Rebecca jumped down and splashed across to them. 'What have you got for us?'

'Bryne here has a broken arm and lots of bruises. His mum needs a nice warm bed for the night in hospital.' Beau gave them a quick rundown.

Fraser led the boy around to the back of the ambulance and helped him aboard, while Rebecca and some of the SAR guys loaded Bryne's mother onto a stretcher.

Finally, Fraser held open the SUV's door. 'Come on, Nikki, let's go home and get dry.'

'Home, as in Mum and Dad's place,' she muttered. 'I don't fancy driving back to town with all that water on the roads.'

Disappointment flooded Fraser. For one crazy moment he'd forgotten they weren't a couple. They weren't even having a relationship so they didn't do things like go home together. 'I guess you're right. It's probably crazy to be on the road tonight if you don't have to be.'

'There's plenty of room for you to stay too,' Nikki murmured, staring fixedly out the windscreen. 'I'm sure Mum will be happy to put you up for the night.'

Warmth trickled through Fraser at the offhand invitation. Three steps forward, none back. Progress?

CHAPTER SEVEN

FRASER pulled into the drive of his parents' home just after six the next morning. He'd left a note on the bench back at Allan and Rose Page's house, thanking them for putting him up the previous night.

Quietly closing the truck door, he headed up the path in the dark to the front door. Hopefully his dad had had a quiet night.

His father's newly querulous voice shattered that wish. 'What do you think you're doing, skulking around here, you scoundrel?'

'Dad? What are you doing outside this early?' Fraser stared at the semi-naked man sitting on the top step. 'You need more than pyjama pants to protect yourself against the cold and damp.' At least the rain had finally stopped.

'Keeping an eye out for you, Henry Broad. You needn't think you're getting past me to

Molly. She's mine now. She don't want a bar of you, so beat it.'

Shock slammed into Fraser, forcing the air out of his lungs. *Dad doesn't recognise me.* Knowing that this would happen didn't lessen the impact or the pain. *He's really lost all sense of what's real.*

'Dad, it's me, your son.' Fraser spoke evenly, quietly, pretending his heart wasn't pounding his ribs like a battering ram. He needed to make his father come back from wherever his mind had wandered. 'Dad, I'm Fraser,' he said as he slipped his jacket off and around his dad's shivering shoulders. This was the man who'd tormented and bullied him all his childhood and yet Fraser would give anything to bring back the father he was more familiar with.

'Go home, Broad.' His dad's voice dipped, wavered, as though he wasn't sure what was going on.

Fraser grimaced. *How long has Dad been out here?* His skin was icy. Hypothermic? Shivering and confusion were symptoms. But the confusion was more likely due to the dementia. 'Come on, let's get you inside and warm.'

Where was Mum? Finally getting a desperately needed full night's sleep? This would rattle her, and cause more sleepless nights as she kept one eye open to watch over the man she'd spent all her adult life with.

His dad stood up slowly. 'Don't get funny with me, Broad. I know you've been sneaking around, trying to win Molly away from me.' He swung an arm in Fraser's direction.

Carefully catching the arm, which wasn't as muscular as it used to be, Fraser tried to turn his father round and lead him inside, all the while aching for this once strong man. The man who'd been a hard father, who'd pushed him around, taunted him over any shortcomings, and yet had sat with him for every single round of chemo.

Twisting out of Fraser's hands, his dad yelled, 'Don't you touch me. Get off my property and don't come back, you hear?'

Fraser reluctantly tried another tack. 'Ken, get your butt in the house now before Molly comes looking for you. She's going to be mad as hell if she finds you out here.' It was a crappy state of affairs when a man had to speak to his father like this, but if it meant getting him inside and wrapped up in warm clothes then it would be worth it.

His father glared at him then suddenly peered sheepishly over his shoulder at the front door as though expecting Molly to appear suddenly. 'She'd give me a bollocking, wouldn't she, son?'

Son. Fraser's heart tripped. *Thank you, Dad.* But there were going to be more and more instances when he wasn't recognised by the man who'd reared him, who'd been the reason he'd left Blenheim. Who'd made him the person he was. Because of his father he'd spent years polishing his skills at beguiling people, bringing them onside so they liked him. But suddenly his eyes moistened. Families were meant to be about loving and caring, whereas he'd always believed his father was an adversary.

With his mum everything had been different, all about love and caring. His dad had bullied her as well, but she'd accepted it, whereas he'd fought back. And won his father's love along the way.

'Come on, Dad.' Taking his father's elbow, Fraser directed him inside, closing the door on the outside world. As he and his mum had done for as long as he could remember.

'Ken? Fraser? What's going on?' His mum came towards them, tying a belt around her robe, looking bewildered. 'Where have you been, Ken? I didn't notice he'd gone,' she added in an aside to Fraser.

'It's all right, Mum. I'll get him dry and dressed in something warm. Maybe you could turn on the heaters and make us all a cup of tea.'

Seeing the weariness in his mother's face made the tears prick harder at the backs of his eyelids. This disease was so unfair. Thank goodness he'd come back to Blenheim when he had. His mum couldn't have managed alone for much longer. Even with him here it wasn't easy, but he knew better than to mention rest homes and dementia units again. She'd send him packing for sure.

Not that Fraser could blame her. If he loved someone as much as his mum loved his dad, despite everything, then he'd be dead set against handing over her care to strangers. A picture of Nikki clambering up the camper van last night slipped into his head, along with the chill he'd known as he'd watched her. He'd feared for her, been terrified something dreadful would happen to her. He'd wanted to be the one on the end of the pulleys and ropes, holding her safe.

Sighing, Fraser dropped a kiss on his mum's wrinkled forehead. 'Who's this Broad character?' he whispered.

'The man your father charmed me away from.' His mum smiled softly, her eyes misty. 'Thank goodness.'

'Really?' Shock rippled through him. He'd never understood how his mum could love his dad despite the bullying and demands he'd made on her. Yet now her face shone with it. She wouldn't change a thing. He could see that in the steel at the back of her eyes, in the hand that rubbed his dad's arm.

'Absolutely.'

'Sorry.' He kissed her soft cheek, knowing she wouldn't understand he was apologising for trying to belittle that love when he'd been a teen and thought he knew everything. But setting Nikki free had been just as loving. In a back-to-front way. Must have picked up some of his mother's good characteristics.

'We all used to go to the dance hall in town and your dad was a better dancer than Henry.'

'I got that skill from him, then.' Fraser was very sorry for hurting his mum, but his parents' relationship was not one he wanted to emulate. Sometimes, in the deep of the night, he worried he'd turn out to be no better than his father. What if he had married Nikki and spent their whole life together putting her endeavours down, humiliating her? What if he'd had all those kids he yearned for and then spent for ever making them wish they'd never been born? Or did love really conquer all those fears?

'Fraser.' His mum's gentle voice cut through his questions. 'Dad needs to get warm. Now.' Her steady gaze said she did understand.

With a brief nod Fraser turned back to his father and took his arm again. 'Come on, Dad.'

To concentrate on helping his parents properly he had to ignore the bubble of anguish that had arrived in his belly when he'd seen his dad sitting outside. This disease was never going away. It was going to end in tears and it was his job to cushion the impact for his mum. All part of resuming his place in his family, in his home town.

* * *

Nikki flipped open her phone, squeezed it between her ear and shoulder, and continued loading the washing machine. 'Hello?'

'It's Fraser.' Two words. Two very tired words.

Her heart stopped. The very person she'd been thinking about. But why was he ringing her? 'What are you up to?'

'Have you been for your run yet?'

Yes, she had, hours ago. But she hesitated. Something in Fraser's tone suggested he desperately needed company. 'I was about to head out. Want to join me?' Two runs in one day would be hard on her legs but she'd manage. Maybe they'd take it easy. As if. Fraser was a regular runner, too, and she already knew how competitive he was at everything.

'I'd like that. Where shall I meet you?' he asked.

'I'll pick you up in ten, if that suits. We can head up to Wither Hills Farm Park.'

'That works perfectly. See you shortly.' Fraser hung up.

Nikki stared at her phone. Something was up, but why had he asked her to go for a run with him? It wasn't as though he told her much about himself these days. They'd managed to make working together possible by not sharing any personal information.

Ten minutes, she'd said. Minus sixty seconds already. Nikki turned the washing machine on and raced to her bedroom for a clean set of track pants and sweatshirt.

At the foot of the Wither Hills Farm Park they did warm-up stretches before running up the track that would eventually edge around the side of the hill. Nikki took the lead. 'Come on, slow-coach,' she taunted over her shoulder. So far Fraser hadn't said a word about why he'd wanted to join her and her nerves were winding tighter by the minute.

'Slowcoach, eh?' Fraser gave a tense smile that didn't reach his eyes as he lengthened his stride to pass her.

Nikki immediately upped her pace, feeling the strain in her calf muscles as she passed Fraser, only to have him tap her shoulder as he raced past her again. At the top of the hill they collapsed against the fence, gasping cold air into their lungs.

Finally, Fraser muttered, 'Next time I have a rush of blood to the head and suggest going for a run with you I'll go to the gym instead. You're very fit.'

'You're not so bad yourself.' Nikki straightened up, hands on hips as she stretched her back. The wind was chilly, rapidly cooling her down.

His gaze cruised over her, slowing at her breasts. 'When did you take up running? You never used to own a pair of sports shoes, let alone know how to use them.'

Embarrassment warmed her cold cheeks. About to avoid the question, she hesitated. One of her biggest complaints about Fraser was that he didn't tell her anything important. Hauling in a lungful of air, she told him, 'After you left me I got depressed. Like really depressed. I had to take drugs for a while.'

The eyes that Fraser turned on her were dark caramel and full of guilt and concern. 'That explains the way you walk now.'

'What?'

'You used to have a spring in your step, as though nothing could keep you down. Your love of life flowed through everything you did.' His gaze remained fixed on her. 'I took that away from you.'

Blimey. He carried so much guilt. She reached a hand out, touched his lightly. 'Don't. It's over now. You've explained and I have the answers I'd been looking for. I have to own some of what happened to me, too.' Could she have prevented the depression? Should she have knocked on Fraser's door and demanded answers, instead of hiding away feeling sorry for herself? She'd never know.

Fraser turned his hand over, laced his fingers with hers, shook his head at her. 'That's too easy.'

Probably. Striving for a lighter tone, she smiled. 'There was nothing easy about taking up running, believe me. I hated it at first, but my doctor kept insisting I not give up.' She pulled her hand free, away from the temptation to hold on tight, to try and find that connection they used to have.

'What kept you going?'

'I'd lost a lot of weight and didn't want to find it again so in the end that's why I persevered. For weeks I ached from top to toe, then one day

I woke feeling great and knew I'd never give up running, or some form of exercise, again.'

'It agrees with you. You look fantastic. But you always did.'

I did? Really? She stared at Fraser, but could see nothing in his eyes that refuted his words. Wow. But it didn't matter what he'd thought, it was still too late. Rubbing her hands up and down her arms, she said, 'Let's walk a bit. It's too cold to stand still.'

Fraser nodded but remained staring out over the town for a long moment. Finally, he turned to her. 'My father's getting worse, and there's not a thing I can do about it. It's like watching a coil of wire unwinding under its own volition. I can't stop it. I can't change anything. And worst of all, it's too late to tell him the things I've wanted to tell him most of my life.'

The helplessness in his eyes caught at her, making her heart ache for him. 'What would you say to him if you could?'

She had to strain to hear his reply. 'I'd tell him I forgive him.'

'I'm sure he knows. You came home for him. That says what words don't.'

Fraser turned to face her. ‘I know he loved me. He just didn’t know how to show it. Until I was ill. Then he spent months with me. Still tried to tell me what to do, though.’ Fraser’s smile was poignant. ‘Guess that’ll never change.’

Nikki asked, ‘So what happened today? Did your dad take a turn for the worse?’

‘When I got home this morning Dad was sitting on the front porch dressed in nothing but his PJ bottoms. He didn’t know me.’ Fraser’s Adam’s apple bobbed and he ran his knuckles down his cheek. ‘Called me Henry Broad. Accused me of trying to steal his wife from him. Turns out Broad’s an old flame of Mum’s. The whole thing would be funny if it wasn’t so damned sad.’

Nikki tossed caution to the wind and stepped in front of him to wrap her arms around him. ‘I can’t begin to imagine how you cope. What about your mother? Is she okay?’

He stood absolutely still, hands at his sides. Waiting for her to let go? She didn’t, instead hugging tighter. This was what friends did, and she could be Fraser’s friend. For now.

Finally, he relaxed into her hold, and his hands came up around her back. Against her cheek he murmured, 'Mum's good. Exhausted, but she's good.'

When they began shivering from the cold he pulled away and began jogging slowly. 'Mum's so patient with him, not to mention stubbornly determined to keep Dad at home with her.'

'How much longer can she realistically do that?' Nikki followed, feeling warm on the inside despite the chill wind making her shiver. A hug with Fraser had lifted her spirits no end.

Fraser shrugged. 'How long's a piece of string? There's no way of knowing with this disease. She swears he's been okay up till now.'

'I bet your mother's just happy you're here now.'

'I guess.' Then he tossed a challenge over his shoulder. 'Last one back to the car buys lunch.' And he was gone, racing down the track like a greyhound.

'If you think I'm buying, think again…' But as she sped down the narrow path after him she knew there was no way he'd let her beat him. It wasn't in his nature.

Fraser hurdled over the last fence and slapped his hand on the vehicle first. 'I won.'

Nikki slipped between the fence wires. 'You cheated.'

His eyes rolled skywards. 'Excuses, excuses.' He opened the car door, leaned his arms on the roof. 'Thanks for coming out with me. I needed to let off steam.'

Nikki gazed into those serious eyes and her breath hitched in her throat. He'd chosen her to spend the morning with when he'd wanted to put the pain of his father's illness out of his mind. That made her feel warm and soft inside. Special, even. Like they were getting close again.

'Nikki.' Fraser strode around the car to her. 'Nikki, I…' His hands gripped her upper arms.

'You wh-what?' There was an unfamiliar yet very familiar look in those beautiful eyes gazing at her. He wanted to kiss her, but he was wary. Heat and longing stared out at her, turned her insides soft, exploding all thought of keeping her distance. Her legs stretched, lifting her onto her toes. Her hands gripped the front of his windbreaker jacket and hauled him closer.

'Kiss me, Fraser,' she demanded, secure in the knowledge he wanted it as much as she suddenly did.

His eyes widened and he grabbed her to him. 'I've missed you,' he murmured against her mouth.

Then his lips covered hers, slick, forcing her mouth wide. His tongue pushed inside, teasing, tasting, dancing with hers. Driving her crazy with desire.

Pressing her body length against Fraser, her breasts hard against his chest, her belly against his, thigh to thigh, excitement wound tightly deep inside her womanhood. She needed to touch his skin. Her hands slipped under his shirt, fingers spreading wide on his back, his skin smooth and warm under her fingertips.

She pressed even closer and he wound his arms tighter around her. His shaft, hard, pressed against her belly. It had been so long since she'd known this need. Every muscle in her body shook as his kisses deepened, became hungrier. Shaking with need for him. She wanted him. She wanted Fraser? Yes.

No. She jerked her mouth free. No. They couldn't do this. She wasn't ready. She'd never be ready for him.

Fraser took her face in his hands. The eyes that

met hers were full of concern and slowly evaporating need. 'You want to stop?'

Unable to speak, she nodded slowly. And bit back the denial threatening to break from her mouth.

He leaned in, placed the softest of soft kisses on each cheek, then her mouth. 'Okay.' And he stepped away, around the SUV to the other side, never taking his gaze off her.

She stared at him, her hands trembling. How could she have let that kiss happen?

How had she stopped it?

As Nikki pulled into the driveway of his parents' home a little later she gasped. 'That's Mum's car. What's she doing here?'

'Seeing if there's anything I can do for Molly and Ken.' Rose Page answered her daughter's question when they went inside. 'Fraser said last night he's going to Christchurch next month for training so I dropped by to see if Molly might want some company or help with the chores while he's away.'

Nikki gaped at her mother. Yesterday, her brothers seemed to have accepted Fraser back into the fold all too easily, and today her mother had turned up to see Molly McCall.

Yeah, and twenty minutes ago who had been kissing Fraser like a starved woman?

Fraser smiled. 'Thanks, Rose.' Then he turned to his mother. 'Where's Dad?'

'Right here.' Mr McCall loomed up in the doorway. 'Just been catching the midday news and weather. Last night's storm did a lot of damage all over the top half of the South Island.'

It seemed that morning's episode of forgetfulness had passed. Until next time. Pain for Fraser lanced Nikki's heart. It must be dreadful never knowing what offbeat thing his dad might do next. Right now, if she hadn't known, she'd never have guessed Mr McCall had dementia.

Did Fraser ever worry he might get dementia? One glance at him, laughing and chatting with everyone, and she'd have to say no.

'They got that campervan out of the river this morning.' Her mum's voice cut through her thoughts. 'It's a mess. All that poor woman's possessions have been under water all night.'

Molly was looking from Fraser to Nikki. She asked in such an innocent voice that had Nikki wondering if she had 'I've just been kissed by your son' written over her face. 'What are you two doing this afternoon?'

'I'm taking Nik out to lunch.'

Nikki shook her head. 'No, you're not.'

His eyes instantly filled with disappointment. 'I thought that was the deal.'

'The deal was the loser shouts lunch. I believe I came second.' A rush of pleasure warmed her as the disappointment cleared and he smiled a toe-curling smile. 'Even if you did cheat.'

'For that I'll buy the wine. Which vineyard do you recommend?'

The sun had at last cleared the sky of clouds and its warm rays made the garden at the vineyard restaurant very appealing to Nikki and Fraser. They selected a table out in the open, away from the shade of the trees.

'This is definitely something I didn't get to do very often in Dunedin.' Fraser stretched his long legs under the table. 'And definitely not at this time of the year.'

'I've never missed those freezing winters, all that snow and ice. I still remember the first year we moved down there. I thought I'd never survive the cold.' Nikki shivered exaggeratedly.

'You used to hate leaving the kitchen where you worked to come home at night.' The intensity in his eyes made her blush with memories of how they'd got warm when she had finally got back to their flat. She reached for her glass, sipped the crisp Sauvignon Blanc and nodded. 'Excellent.'

'It is.'

Finally, Fraser looked away, and she was able to draw a full breath. So many good times between them. All ruined by one thing. She shivered. Time to take a break from the past and enjoy this time with Fraser, enjoy today. Leaning back in her chair, Nikki looked around the garden.

'The daffodils are in bud. And over the fence there's green showing on the grapevines. Spring is definitely on the way.' The new growth always lifted her spirits. It was like a new beginning. Was that what was happening here with Fraser? Was that what she wanted?

I don't know. But I'm not uncomfortable with him any more.

'Can I take your orders?' A waitress hovered at her elbow and Nikki refocused, ordering the smoked salmon terrine and salad.

Fraser leaned his elbows on the table and studied her over his clasped hands. 'Don't you miss the kitchen at all?'

'I miss putting together a beautiful meal that someone's paying for and therefore expecting the best. I miss being around other foodies all the time. But the daily grind of producing the same thing over and over, of not being able to be creative?' She shook her head. 'I'd rather strap an oxygen mask on a seriously ill asthmatic patient and save their life.'

'Maybe you should've been the one going to med school. There's room for more than one doctor in your family.'

'I don't think so.' Between her fingers her glass twisted back and forth. 'Would you ever consider finishing your degree? I can't accept you won't ever become a doctor.'

'Funny thing, but since I've come home on a permanent basis I've started thinking about that and wondering if I should try and qualify. But I'm not sure I want to go into debt for it when

Mum's going to be paying huge fees for Dad to go into a rest home soon.' When she opened her mouth he held his hand up. 'Nik, it's not possible. I've said I'll be around for Mum now that Dad's ill. I won't break that promise. Or any others I get to make in the future.'

'Fair enough.'

'I meant that, Nik.' He was watching her with wide eyes, as though he might miss any nuances in her expression. 'I'm done with letting down the people I care about.'

'I believe you.' *I doubt I'd trust you with my heart again, but I believe you mean what you say.* She deliberately returned to his medical career. 'So you've signed on for life at the Blenheim station, then.'

He blinked, turned that intense gaze away. 'I hadn't thought of it like that. Just as well I really enjoy being a paramedic. It's edgy, fun and helping people in stressful situations. Which reminds me, have you heard how Charlotte's getting on?'

'She's out of her coma but the doctors aren't saying yet if she'll be all right.'

'How are Mark and Ella? I can't imagine what they're going though.'

'They've moved into a motel unit next to the hospital, and George is with them now.' When Fraser's eyebrows lifted in query she added, 'George is their son. He's two years younger than Charlotte.'

'Weird how things turn out. Mark and Ella couldn't stand each other at school, yet now they're married with kids and helping each other through what has to be the worst time of their lives.'

Yes, they're sticking together, sharing the pain. 'They've grown closer and closer over the years since they married. Charlotte came along before they married, and Ella always says that was the best thing that could have happened to them. She brought them together.'

Wariness slipped into Fraser's eyes, but he didn't say anything, just let her carry on talking.

'I hope more than anything Charlotte makes it.' *I worry that there was something more I could've done to save her.*

'We did our best, Nik. You were awesome with her.'

‘I’m that obvious?’

‘You forget how well I used to know you.’ His smile was tender, almost sad.

‘No, I haven’t forgotten.’ It was time to return the conversation to safer ground. Sitting up straighter, she looked around. ‘I wonder where our meals have got to.’

The meals were scrumptious when they arrived. ‘Want a second wine?’ Fraser asked as they put down their knives and forks.

‘Yes, it’s so lovely out here I’m not ready to leave.’ And now that they’d managed to talk about everyday things for a while she’d relaxed even more with Fraser.

‘Two glasses of Sauvignon Blanc for two of my favourite people.’

Fraser looked up into the face of Isabella Fowler. He leapt up and grabbed her in a hug. ‘How are you?’

‘I’m good.’ Isabella hugged him back then moved to Nikki, hugging her extra tight. ‘I hope you were going to poke your head into the kitchen before you left.’ She grinned at Nikki. ‘Got a spare apron if you’re tired of saving people.’

Nikki laughed. 'Not yet. Anyway, there was never room for both of us in your kitchen.'

'You worked here?' Fraser stared at Nikki. 'You didn't say.'

'Why do you think I chose this restaurant?'

Isabella sat down between them. 'I heard about your dad, Fraser. I'm sorry. Is that why you're back home?'

'One of the reasons.' He quickly changed the subject, not wanting to talk about the past and knowing how Isabella wouldn't hesitate to ask awkward questions. One thing he'd learned growing up next door to her was that nothing but nothing was a secret with her. 'Are you head chef here?'

'I own the restaurant, along with my partner, André, from Paris.' Her face filled with love. 'He drove into town one day, had a meal at the bistro I worked at and the rest is history.'

'She tied André from Paris down so he couldn't leave.' Grinning, Nikki turned to Isabella. 'Or did you remove the sparkplugs from that old clanger he drove? I can't remember.'

Isabella touched her nose with a forefinger. 'I had my ways.' Then she went on, 'I'm glad to see you two out together. I never understood why you split.'

Fraser saw the instant denial in Nikki's eyes and rushed in to save her from more difficult questions Isabella was capable of tossing up. 'We're not back together, just having lunch. I work on the ambulances too.'

Thankfully, a waitress appeared. 'Isabella, you're needed in the kitchen. André's arguing about a delivery.'

She jumped up. 'I'd better sort this out. André's not known for his patience. Great to see you two. And if you can, work on getting back together. I'd love to dance at your wedding.'

The silence was deafening. Fraser stared into the depths of his glass, waiting for Nikki to explode. When she didn't he looked up slowly and was taken aback by the look of shock on her face.

'She's too much, isn't she?' he tendered.

'Yep.' Nik nodded. 'Way out there.'

So what do you think about Isabella's suggestion? Is it too awful to contemplate? He took a mouthful of his wine. 'Of course, there's a lot she doesn't know.'

Nik's mouth flattened into a line. 'Can I ask you something?'

Why did his stomach tighten? 'Sure.'

'Are you really home for good? When your dad's in care and your mum no longer needs your help, won't you want to leave again? Go back to university or Dunedin?' Her finger scratched at a knot in the wood of the tabletop.

His heart slowed, settled heavily. Nikki still didn't trust him one hundred per cent. He wouldn't have minded too much if he hadn't kissed her again and finally woken up to the fact that he loved her, had never stopped loving her. He'd done a damned fine job of hiding his feelings from himself, but they were only lurking in the dark recesses of his mind, waiting to pounce on him when he least expected it.

'I'm really home for good,' he reiterated. 'I'm no longer that teen who left Blenheim to get away from things I couldn't face. I've learned family and friends are more important than anything. And this is where they are.'

'I see.' Her tone held too much doubt for that to be true.

CHAPTER EIGHT

NIKKI stopped two metres from the door into Gavin and Patricia's leaving party, apprehension suddenly gripping her, twisting her stomach. 'Mistletoe? In September? Who's dumb idea is that?'

As if she couldn't guess. Standing directly beneath the green, plastic ornament with its tiny white berries, Fraser looked too darned smug for his own good, waiting to kiss every female going through that door. He looked too darned good for her equilibrium.

Unbelievable how much she'd missed him while he'd been in Christchurch. Work hadn't been the same without him in the truck beside her, those all-seeing brown eyes not there watching her, without his easy way of cheering up patients.

I missed Fraser. What did it mean? She couldn't quite accept his assurances that he wouldn't be leaving some time in the future and that kept a brake on her delving too deeply into what she might want with Fraser.

Beside her Amber giggled. 'It's great. Only Fraser would come up with this idea. He's also the only man on the staff worth kissing. As I'm sure you are aware.'

Very. But she couldn't begrudge him a few kisses with all the women. She had no right to exclusivity. They weren't a couple. Dang. Her mouth watered. Dressed in jeans that must've taken hours to squeeze those muscular thighs and tight butt into and a black open-necked shirt that exposed just enough chest to make her fingers itch, Fraser was the best sight she'd seen since—since she'd last seen him more than a week ago. At that moment Fraser turned round from charming the newest recruit and smiled at them. 'Hey, ladies, welcome to Christmas in spring. Slip those jackets off and come in.'

Amber nudged past her, digging an elbow into her waist. 'Come on. This is fun.'

Fraser didn't notice Amber. His eyes were appraising Nikki slowly. Too darned slowly. As if he might've missed her too. Had he? Nikki sucked her stomach in, tugged her shoulders back. And stepped forward. 'Evening, Fraser. How'd the course go?'

'Nik, we're not talking work tonight. But I'm glad you're here. I'd have had to pull down the mistletoe if you hadn't made it.' A slow-burning smile lifted his mouth, caressed and teased her.

'You don't think you've got your seasons muddled up?' Her return smile was slow and wide and caressed him back. Blimey, she couldn't believe how good it was to be with him. Ten days since she'd last worked with him and she was slobbering like a puppy.

Used to be you never wanted to see him again.

'Only way to get a kiss from you so early on in the evening.'

'You're flirting with me.' Double dang. This was over the top. Be truthful. There were too many days when she felt a strong pull towards him. The fierce physical attraction she'd felt that first day had not gone away, instead gnawing at her like a dog did at a bone. The fierce physical attraction she'd had for him since her teen years. Her brain and her body had regularly been at loggerheads over Fraser. Even more so now, when she knew better than to give in to his look that turned her knees to something with the strength of syrup.

'If it works,' he murmured.

Amber tapped his shoulder. 'I'm waiting for my mistletoe treat.'

Fraser blinked, finally pulled those potent, earthy eyes away from Nikki. Draping an arm over Amber's shoulder, he dropped a light kiss on her cheek.

Amber chuckled loudly. 'Aw, shucks. I guess you're saving the best for Nikki.'

Nikki scowled, suddenly afraid of where her emotions were taking her. On a ride to nowhere with Fraser? She'd be safer going home and washing her already clean hair. She may have forgiven him but she was not ready for anything more than the two kisses they'd already shared.

'Nikki, come on.' Amber's voice boomed across the gap from where she was hanging up her jacket inside the room decorated with red and green baubles and streamers. 'Give Fraser a smacker of a kiss. All in the party spirit, of course.'

Shrugging out of her jacket, Nikki made to

step through the doorway and was stopped slap bang in the middle by two firm hands on her shoulders. Under her top her skin tingled. Her heartbeat went into overdrive. Great. So much for regaining control over her hormones.

'Not so fast, Nikki.' His deep yet soft voice stroked her, cranked up the heat in her skin.

Her stomach twisted tighter than a knotted rope. Her teeth jarred as her mouth snapped shut. But her heart seemed to clap encouragement to her brain for the crazy ideas suddenly forming about kissing those full lips just inches away. Forget keeping her distance. She suddenly wanted to be close to Fraser. Again.

'You okay?' he asked softly, too softly. His words caressed her cheek, squeezed her stomach, sent her senses spiralling with desire.

Help. She gulped. 'Why wouldn't I be?' she asked in a strange, childlike voice, while trying to ignore that sexy light stubble accentuating his strong chin.

'How have you been?' Fraser's full mouth curved into a sweet, friendly smile. A harmless smile. Or was it beguiling? His eyes twinkled at her. 'I missed you.' He lowered his head towards hers and gently pulled her close, then those intriguing lips were caressing hers. In a tantalising, erotic way. Soft yet demanding, pliant yet strong.

Nikki couldn't have moved if someone had yelled, 'Fire!' Her senses filled with the scent of Fraser's aftershave; subtle and alluring. Her shoulders felt branded where his fingers pressed. His breathing was light and quick. Her lips felt the manliness of his lips, and her mouth opened under his.

Big mistake. Kisses weren't meant to be so diverting, so dangerous. *Pull away.* She would. In a moment. One more second of tasting this man. Of feeling his lips, his tongue. Oh, wow, nothing, no previous kisses had prepared her for the weightlessness overtaking her now. Nothing had prepared her for the sheer need crawling up through her bones, her muscles, through every cell. Fraser was back.

'Hey, you two, mind if we come in?'

Nikki leapt backwards, out of Fraser's embrace, her face turning scarlet. And stared into Mike's grinning face.

'Glad to see you've patched up your differences,' Mike added. 'Fraser, I don't think you've met my wife.'

Nikki escaped, going to sit at a table with Amber, who pushed a glass towards her. 'Vodka with a twist to cool you down after that hot smooch.'

'Danged mistletoe.' She gulped a large mouthful.

'And absolutely nothing to do with the hottest guy here, of course.' Amber grinned.

Nikki turned away as yet more heat scorched her cheeks. Her eyes found Fraser, latched onto him as he headed over to the jukebox. His strides were confident, the swing of his arms relaxed. Her tongue traced the edges of her lips, tasting him. The urge to run her fingers through his hair shining in the gleam from the rotating disco lights was sudden and fierce.

'His choice is perfect for dancing,' she muttered as music suddenly filled the hall. Her feet began tapping the rhythm as it filled her ears.

Amber grinned. 'He knows his stuff.'

Tell me about it. My blood's zinging around my body. My heart rate's so high it's danger-

ous. Again Nikki's tongue traced her lips. 'And doesn't he know it.'

Amber stood up. 'Let's start dancing. We'll get everyone on the floor and make this party rock.'

'Good idea.' Better than ogling Fraser. Nikki looked around and her eyes locked with Fraser's as he moved towards her.

'Want to dance?' he asked, the intensity in his gaze rocking her back on her heels. 'You used to enjoy dancing.'

The floor tilted dangerously. 'You remember.'

His hand caught her elbow for the second time tonight. Without the barrier of her thick jacket his touch scorched her, dried her mouth. 'I remember a lot of things.'

Before Nikki could ask what, she was swung around in Fraser's arms and danced across the floor. The words dried in her throat as his arms held her effortlessly and his thighs pushed against hers to direct her in their dance. She hadn't danced like this since quitting the ballroom-dancing team at the same time she'd left Dunedin. And Fraser had been the only dancing partner who'd held her as though she might break. And the only man who'd made her want to shimmy in his arms so she could feel his hands move over her skin.

The tempo of the music changed and Nikki reluctantly slipped out of his arms. Wriggling her hips, she was totally aware of him watching her with thought-diverting intensity. Her skin melted, her mouth tasted like a desert, and deep inside a hot, raw need poured through her. Desire so intense she thought she was about to explode.

'I could do with a cold drink.' She turned, pushed through the other dancers, making her way to the table where she glugged down the rest of her vodka.

'Like another of those?' Fraser asked from beside her.

She blinked. 'I'll make it a lemonade this time.' Sinking down onto a chair, hands clasped tightly in her lap, she watched him skirting the crowd as he strode purposefully towards the temporary bar, barely stopping to talk to anyone who tried to waylay him. As if he was focused on looking out for her, and no one else mattered.

'Idiot,' Fraser muttered. 'Why the hell did I go and kiss Nikki like that? Here? Now? So much for trying to win her back by taking things slowly.'

The devil of it was once he'd started he hadn't been able to stop. Who knew what would've happened if Mike hadn't arrived at that moment? He'd been lost in her. Her scent that reminded him of summer gardens, her beautiful face and stunning figure, that mass of shining hair spilling down her back. She was something else. Roasting hot. So sexy it was a wonder every man here wasn't queuing up to dance with her. Except he'd beaten them all to her, unable to stay away.

'Something else you've got in common with Nikki—talking to yourself.' Gavin winked at him.

Fraser winced. 'Only way of getting the answers I want.' Not.

'Our Nikki stirring your blood, is she?' When Fraser gaped at him, Gavin added, 'I presume that's who you're muttering about.'

Was he that obvious? 'Need a hand here? I'm not into dancing all night.'

Gavin's eyebrows rose. 'Really? With those moves? Go away.'

'I guess that's a no, then.' Fraser picked up the drinks and headed for Nikki to hand hers over before going to socialise with someone else.

Instead, he sat down right beside her, unable to walk away. He looked up at the ceiling to see if there was a puppeteer pulling his strings. Nope. Dropping his head, his gaze clashed with Nikki's wide stare. Those azure eyes teasing, heating him, reminding him of making love to her after other dance nights. Dragging his eyes away from temptation, he noted the tension in her upright stance and her tight shoulders as she leaned back to put some distance between them. But the message in her eyes was in direct contrast to her body posture. That kiss had got to her too. Silently, he waved a mental fist in the air. Yes.

'Want to dance some more?' His feet were tapping in time to the music, his body humming with this muscle-tightening need to be holding her. To have her in his arms, to touch her, feel her sexy body moving in time to the music.

'No, thanks.' But she was already standing up, balancing easily in those knee-high black boots with heels that were taller than him. His brain short-circuited. The air got hotter when his gaze cruised up from the boots, over her thighs clad in black stockings to the edge of a very short denim skirt. Up to layers of tight-fitting tops that accentuated her stunning curves.

Nikki Page. The girl who'd haunted his sleep for years. All the times he'd cried for her, for them, when life had got too tough to handle alone. He'd never been able to let her go from his heart, from his soul.

'You happy to sit there like an old man?' Nik stood, hands on hips, smiling down at him. His breath stuck in his throat. Her skirt and boots showcased those stunning legs. A few extra kilos used to cover her hips and he wished she hadn't lost them. All that running she did had thinned her down too much. But she was still so lovely he wanted to weep.

'Or do you want to dance with someone else?'

He heard the surprising hurt in her voice, knew she still held deep concerns over her attractiveness. Because of him. He jumped up and grabbed her hand. 'Old man, eh? You're so going to regret that comment by the end of the night.'

A new tune filled the air, a much slower pace

than they'd had for a while. Nikki glanced up into Fraser's eyes and stilled.

His gaze was fixed on her, so intense, so full of something she wasn't sure she should believe. Desire. For her. Slowly shaking her head from side to side, she tried to step back.

His hands were on her waist, holding her, pulling her so close she had to tip her head back to keep watching him, his gaze obliterating all thought processes. His face came slowly closer and closer until his lips brushed her forehead, down her nose and, at last, her mouth. Her lips were trembling as she pushed up on to her toes to get more of his mouth. Her hands gripped his shoulders. To hold him as near as possible. To hold her upright on suddenly lifeless legs.

Fraser's mouth stole across hers, opening on her lips. His hands slid around her back and he hauled her in against him so close she could feel all of him. His chest was rock solid under her breasts. His thighs were hard muscle against hers. His rigid reaction to her pressed firmly into her belly.

Someone bumped into them. 'Sorry, guys.' Amber laughed.

Nikki jerked back, glanced around the room. No one else seemed to be taking the slightest bit of notice of them.

'Let's go somewhere quieter,' Fraser murmured by her ear.

She nodded, her tongue suddenly glued to the roof of her mouth. She wanted more of that kiss. It would be so unfair to stop now. Her fingers laced with Fraser's as they sped to the door and out into the hall's entry area, where he stopped their hasty retreat and picked up where he'd left off kissing her.

Her mind sparked and melted. All reason disappeared in a heartbeat. Her body became liquid, moving only to keep her lips pressed to Fraser's, to keep her breasts rubbing against his chest, to hold him tight.

'Nikki,' he murmured against her mouth. 'You're driving me insane.'

Welcome to her world. Insane about described it. Wonderfully, beautifully, sexily crazy. She was in Fraser's arms and she did not want to back off. The tiniest warning sounded somewhere inside her skull, but she shoved it aside and focused entirely on kissing Fraser. Sliding her tongue across his lips, she sought his taste, his mouth. Their tongues danced around each other, teasing, promising, rediscovering.

He slipped his hands up to her face, held her closer, his eyes slumberous with yearning. For her? Suddenly he tore his mouth away and snatched her hand. 'Come on. We need privacy.'

They ducked into a tiny room off to the side and Fraser banged the door shut, sliding the lock into place. Then he leaned back against the door and lifted Nikki into his arms. Stretching up on her toes, teetering on the tips of her boots, she ran her fingertips across his mouth.

Fraser groaned as she slipped each finger over his bottom lip. He sucked them into his mouth, rolled his tongue over their pads. Needles of desire zipped through her hands, up her arms and spread out over her body, bringing every nerve ending to life, awakening her body.

He turned her round so she leaned back against his body. His hands slipped under all her tops up to her bra, pushing beneath the lacy fabric to find her nipples.

Nikki sucked a breath through her teeth at the onslaught of raw longing slamming into her, pounding her. Her nipples were exquisitely tight under the ministrations of his thumbs. Two small peaks, one massive wave of heat rolling through her. How much more of this could she take without melting into a puddle?

Frazer nibbled a line of soft, teasing bites down her neck, making her back arch and pushing her breasts further into his hands. Against her backside pressed his need for her, hard and strong, insistent.

'Fraser?' she croaked.

His mouth stilled, his body tensed. 'Yes?' he breathed against her skin.

'Don't stop.' What had she really been going to say? Her mind had gone blank, taken over by a growing sense of urgency.

His groan excited her further. 'For a moment there you had me worried.' He spun her round, his hands sliding from her breasts to her sides to her back, then down over her buttocks, taking his time to savour every cell on the way. 'Your skin's so soft, like satin.'

Was that a good thing? Must be. His tone sounded hungry.

'And firm muscles.' Excitement ramped up in

his voice. 'Very firm.' His mouth trailed a line of moist kisses down the side of her mouth to her neck to her cleavage.

Nikki straightened under his touch, tried to undo the buttons of her tops, and when they wouldn't go through the holes she gave up and tugged the offending garments over her head, dropping them at her feet.

Fraser unclipped her bra with one hand, his other busy teasing a nipple and driving her to the edge of the precipice. Her legs shook as she reached for the buckle of his belt. When his manhood sprang free she wrapped her fingers around it.

'Niiikkiii.' Her name fell slowly off his tongue as his eyes widened, his fingers trembling on her skin. There had been times when this moment had only been a fantasy in his mind, when he'd been afraid it would never happen again, especially not with Nikki. But now it was real. She was here, and in his arms. Fraser let out a sigh.

With her free hand Nikki pushed those tight jeans down enough to make it easier for her to hold all of his sex.

Fraser gasped, his body shuddering. She loved

the power she had over him at this moment. And then he was picking her up, pressing her against the wall, pushing her skirt up to her waist and tugging her panties aside. His fingers slid across her moist centre, stroking her slowly, slowly. Then faster and faster until it seemed she was floating.

The tension grew inside her, tightening, twisting, filling her to the point she thought she'd explode with need. Suddenly her body rocked against his hand as she split in two.

Then Fraser entered her, hard and strong, hot and slick. And when he cried out his passion it was her name on his lips.

Stunned, Fraser let Nikki down so her boots reached the floor. Her uneven breath heated his chest. Her hands trembled on his waist.

She tipped her head back to peer up at him. 'What just happened?'

Her eyes, usually light, were darker, bigger and dazed. His heart jolted, banged his ribs. His hold tightened, brought her so near it was as though they were one. 'I don't know.' But he did know he wanted to do it again. Soon. When he got his breath back, when his body had the strength to begin all over again.

Her cheek settled on his chest. She had always done that afterwards.

He returned to running his thumb over the exposed skin on her lower back. Silky skin, warm skin. Nikki's skin.

On his waist her fingers were pressing softly, one after the other as though playing a tune on a piano. A sensual tune that had a direct line to his libido. Not possible. It was too soon. He'd hardly begun to recover. But south of his waist his body hadn't heard of restraint, didn't realise it was supposed to take a break before coming out to play again.

Under his hands Nikki's body swayed, moving softly left then right, as though to get maximum sensation from his hands. Shock delighted him. Nikki was more than ready for a repeat performance.

Lowering his head, his lips found hers, softly swollen from his kisses. As his tongue swept across them then delved inside her sweet mouth, she groaned and all but climbed into him.

He rocked as the hot sensations clawed at his

gut, at his manhood. This was unbelievable, this was Nikki. This brought hope for the first time in years.

CHAPTER NINE

STANDING under the jets of hot water, rinsing the shampoo out of her hair, Nikki felt drained of energy. Her emotions had been through a blender and were now all mixed up and messy ever since the night of the party.

She'd had sex with Fraser. Twice. And loved every exquisite, nerve-tightening, sweet moment.

Which was the problem.

Because she wanted more. But…

But.

They weren't getting back together. She needed to know he'd always be open and honest in the future. Going by how she had to drag things about the past out of him still, she didn't feel confident that he'd always do that.

He'd had five years to get in touch and tell her why he had walked away. He needn't have waited for the all-clear to do that. Had it never occurred to him that she'd needed closure, had a load of self-doubt that only he could dispel by telling her the truth?

No. Obviously it hadn't.

But.

She'd missed him when he'd gone to that course in Christchurch. She'd enjoyed working alongside him since he'd returned. She even joked with him now. And since the party a fortnight ago neither of them had referred to what had happened between them. It was as though it hadn't happened. Weird. Like the tension between them since Fraser had joined the Blenheim staff had evaporated in a cloud of passion. Weird.

Yet there was still tension deep within her. How could there not be? Dang, she'd made love with him. Twice. More than enough to crank up the fires of desire smouldering inside her.

I will not be distracted. I want more than great sex. I need to know he will always be there for me. And I don't.

She suddenly shivered. The water had gone cold. How long had she been in the shower? Fraser had distracted her.

Outside the shower she sniffed. Something was burning. The brownie. Snatching her towel, she wrapped it around her as she raced for the kitchen. Her cellphone rang. The smoke alarm shrieked a warning.

'Okay, okay, I'm coming.' Tugging on an oven mitt, she quickly took the offending cake from the oven and dumped it in the sink.

Hunting in the utensil drawer for the rolling pin while answering her phone, she swore silently. Yet again she'd ruined something she was cooking because of Fraser.

'Hello?' She spoke into the phone as she jabbed the off button on the alarm.

'Hey, girlfriend, what took you so long? I haven't interrupted anything going on between you and lover boy, have I?' Amber giggled.

'How many times do I have to tell you not to call him that?' Amber didn't have a clue what had happened in that storeroom at the party. Did she?

'As many as it takes to convince me nothing's going on between you two. And considering the way Fraser's always looking at you as though you're the best thing since cellphones were invented, I'd say you haven't got a chance.'

'Thanks, *pal*. It takes two, you know.'

Amber only laughed. 'Did you know it was Mike's birthday?'

'Yes, and I've just burnt the brownie. I'll have to go shopping for more chocolate drops, cocoa and eggs.'

'How many cooking debacles is that since Fraser turned up?'

'Too many.'

Amber's tone changed. 'Nikki? You are all right, aren't you? It's just that you've been very distracted all week. I'll stop teasing you if Fraser is becoming a problem.'

The real concern in her friend's voice brought tears to her eyes. 'I'm fine. He is a problem of sorts but nothing I can't handle.' One way or another. 'After I've been shopping and made more brownies. Tell the guys I'll be in with a treat later this morning.'

Fraser clicked off the online ambulance service study site and rubbed his eyes. 'That's doing my head in.'

'How's this assignment going?' Mike asked.

'Not too bad. Doing the practical course last month certainly helped make sense of it all. Sometimes I think the trainers deliberately make the online notes hard to follow.'

'Wait until you take your practical exam. Then you'll really see how difficult they can make it.'

'I was afraid of that.' On the chair Fraser stretched his hands behind his head and touched his feet to the wall at the back of the desk.

'You'll hose in. You know your stuff, and don't get in a flap on the job. As long as you show that, you'll be an AP in no time.'

Then what? He wouldn't be working alongside Nikki. They'd each have their own crew. Although it made sense not to waste resources, the thought saddened him. Working with Nik was fun. He appreciated her knowledge and skills on the job. This wasn't about loving her. This was about having found something new that they both enjoyed doing.

'Hey, happy birthday, Mike,' the woman right now churning his brain to mush said from the doorway. 'I've brought something for your lunch.'

Watching Nik as she crossed to their boss and gave him a hug, Fraser sighed. She was downright gorgeous. And confident about her role here as an AP and in her colleagues' lives. She was more relaxed with him these days, despite their hot night in the storeroom. Would they ever get back that easy, loving relationship they'd once had? Or was he destined to watch her from the sidelines?

Mike took the proffered cake tin, tugged off the lid. 'Brownies? My favourite.'

'Any cake's your favourite.' Nikki flicked his arm before filling the kettle.

Amber asked, 'Coffee, everyone?' After a chorus of requests she lined up six mugs and spooned in coffee and sugar.

Nikki sat at the table and glanced his way. 'Did you hear Charlotte's coming back to Wairau Hospital tomorrow?'

He sat up. 'Really? That's fantastic news. Isn't it?'

'The best. She still needs a lot of care and rehabilitation but the Wellington doctors think it's best she gets that here now that she's on the mend. She'll be able to see friends and other family members. Ella and Mark are thrilled.'

'I bet they are.'

The phone rang in Mike's office. 'Don't touch that brownie till I get back.'

Then Mike charged back. 'Fraser, turn your phone on. That was the police. It's your father. He's gone missing.'

'What? Dad's missing?' Fraser's stomach churned. Tugging his phone out of his back pocket, he stabbed the keys. 'When did I turn this off?' One ring and his mum answered. 'Mum, what's happening? How long's Dad been missing? I'm on my way.' He barely gave her time to answer before snapping the phone shut, his face grim.

Nikki stood in front of him. 'I'm coming with you.'

Of course she would. 'Mum only noticed Dad wasn't there when she went to get him for breakfast. He could've been gone for hours.'

As Fraser headed out the door, Nikki grabbed his hand. 'I'll ring my mother on the way. She can sit with Molly while this is going on.'

His fingers tightened around hers as they ran

to his vehicle. His heart thudded against his ribs. Where could his dad be? What had been going on in that warped mind today? 'Dad, give me a clue, will you? I need to find you. For Mum's sake. For mine.'

Nikki stayed with Fraser as he ran up the footpath at his parents' home and hauled Molly into a tight hug. Her heart broke all over again as he gently wiped the tears from his mother's face.

'I'll find him, Mum. I promise.'

Stepping forward, Nikki also hugged her. 'Mum's on her way to keep you company. And Dad's going to join the searchers.'

'Thanks, Nikki.' Molly squeezed her tight. 'Stay with Fraser, won't you?'

'Try keeping me away.' She smiled softly then turned to dash back into Fraser's truck just as he banged it into gear.

He raced down the drive, along Redwood Street, taking the first road on their left. His head flicked from side to side as he searched. His foot lifted from the accelerator as he peered down driveways then pressed down, making the little truck surge forward, only to slow again.

'Fraser, you look on the right, I'll take the left.'

'Makes sense.' The truck raced forward, stopped.

'And maybe go easy on the pedal,' she added quietly as her head jerked forward and her neck cricked, doubting he'd take any notice. She refrained from pointing out that they should stop and make a plan, approach this in small increments, not race around like headless chooks.

But Fraser would only tell her she didn't know what she was talking about. Which, in terms of the fear and worry for his dad, she didn't. But she did know her heart was hurting for him, that she wanted to make everything right for him. And there just wasn't much she could do.

Tugging her phone from her pocket, Nikki called Jay. 'We need help.'

Fraser lurched the car around a corner, the tyres squealing. 'Where the hell would he go? Damn it, now Mum has to listen to reason and put Dad into care.'

'Jay's already on his way. SAR has been notified. Blake's with Dad.'

'Right.' Fraser's head was still flipping back and forth, left and right, as he drove down the road. Not trusting her to look as carefully as he did? Fair enough. She'd probably do the same.

'Want me to drive so you can concentrate on looking out the window?' *Before we crash into something.*

'No, I'm fine.'

'Then slow down. Please.' Nikki squinted at an old man disappearing around the corner of a house. Too short to be Ken McCall. 'Fraser, think about places your dad used to go, places that were important to him. Where did he work?'

'The sawmill, which is too far away for him to have walked to, then the building centre.' Fraser did a U-turn. 'Might as well check it out. Nothing else to go on.'

'What about sport? Did he go to Lansdowne Park to watch rugby? The racecourse? Which was his favourite pub? Did he go fishing?'

More than an hour later they'd drawn a blank at every site Fraser could think of. 'Call Jay, find out where they're searching and where we should go next.' Despair filled Fraser's voice. 'Because I'm right out of ideas.'

'We're doing a house-by-house, street-by-street search out from Ken and Molly's property,' Jay informed her. 'You two could try town, see if he's in a café or wandering around the shops. The police are combing the river banks.'

A chill lifted bumps on Nikki's arms. *Please, not the river.* 'Keep us posted.'

They drove up and down every street in the centre of town, peering at people and in shop doors. Nikki jumped out and looked into every café with the same result. Ken McCall had vanished.

Fraser pulled over, the engine idling. His fingers tapped the steering-wheel, his head tilted back against the headrest. 'Gawd, Nik, what if I don't find him? What if—?' He choked off the next words.

'Don't even think that,' she chided gently. 'He's out there somewhere and half the town's searching for him. It's only a matter of time.' If only she believed herself. A vision of the police on the river banks flashed up in her head, and she bit down on the cry threatening to break from her throat. That wouldn't help Fraser at all.

'Let's be realistic, Nik. Anything could've happened to him.'

His sharp tone pierced her but she continued

anyway. 'At least it's a warm, late-spring day, not like that time you found him on the steps in his PJs.'

'The day he mistook me for Henry Broad.'

Nikki spun around to stare at him.

Fraser's head snapped forward.

'That's it,' they cried in unison.

'It has to be, please,' Nikki whispered.

Fraser snatched his phone and punched redial. 'Mum? Where was that dance hall you used to meet Dad at?'

A week later, after they'd found his dad dressed in his suit and tie, standing on the old site where the hall used to be, Fraser backed the ambulance into the garage and turned off the engine. The door rattled down and he winced. 'That should wake Chloe and Ryan.'

'Serve them right for having a perfect shift so far. And since it's just gone four they're very unlikely to get a call now.' Nikki yawned. 'There are advantages to being on truck two during the night.'

'Feel like a hot drink? Or do you want to get some shut-eye?' He could do with her company, even so early in the morning. He was unable to explain it, but ever since his dad's disappearing act he'd felt like this, wanting to spend as much time as possible with Nikki.

Nik turned those tired but beautiful eyes on him. 'Tea would be great. There might even be a slice of coffee cake in the pantry to go with it.'

'At this hour?' He jumped out and went to plug the power supply into the ambulance.

'I'll run it off before lunch.' At the supply room she tapped in the security code and opened the door. 'I'll replace the drugs and equipment if you're boiling the jug.'

Handing Nik a steaming mug ten minutes later, Fraser sank into one of the armchairs and stretched out, crossed his feet. 'What've you got planned for your days off?'

She dropped into the chair beside him. 'Not a lot. Probably go out to the farm one of the days. What about you?'

'Driving Mum and Dad to Nelson tomorrow. They're staying at a hospital unit while Dad's assessed for placement in rest-home care.'

Nikki sighed. 'That must be really hard for you

and Molly.' She sipped her tea and studied him over the rim. 'But no surprise, huh?'

'Not after the other day's event. Even Mum admits it's time, but she's not liking it one bit. I can't blame her. It will be hard, a bit like separating yet not really.'

Her brow furrowed. 'Does this mean Ken's going to be living in Nelson?'

'No way. But all the assessments are done there at the moment. Mum's found a place here for him that'll be available before Christmas.'

'Christmas. That's not too far away. Surely you can have Ken at home for that?'

'That'll be up to Mum.' Fraser swallowed some tea. 'She just wants to get this assessment out of the way before making too many plans.' It wasn't going to be easy, even though he knew this was the right thing to do for his father.

'Want me to come with you tomorrow?' Nik's soft voice covered him like a blanket, soothing out the tension in his shoulders, warming the cold place in his heart.

'I'd love you to.' It would be so much easier having someone to share the day with, to make that trip back from Nelson with. He was done with trying to do things alone. Especially if Nik was offering to be there for him. 'Thanks.'

'If I've ever earned a beer, it's this one.' Fraser groaned. 'What is it with women and shopping? There can't be an outfit left in town.'

'Get over yourself.' Nikki smiled happily.

Fraser had finally relaxed. After an hour with doctors and nursing staff they'd left his parents at the medical unit that dealt with dementia patients, his mother tearfully shooing them away. 'Go. I'll be all right. It's only for three nights. And think of the sleep I'll get with the nurses watching over your father.'

After promising Fraser a beer if she could take a peek in the shops, Nikki had dragged him around town and loaded his arms with parcels.

Finally, he'd growled, 'That's it. Time for that drink you promised. How many new clothes can you wear at one time anyway?'

She laughed. 'That's a man comment. There's no such thing as too many pairs of boots. Or too many clothes. Come on, drink time.' Despite the reason for being in Nelson she was enjoying herself. Fraser was always good company and hopefully she'd managed to cheer him up for a while.

'So there are some perks to being a pack horse.'

'A few small ones.' She tucked her hand around his elbow and stretched her stride to equal his long one.

Just like old times.

She gasped. Yes, it was, wasn't it? Being together, ribbing each other, going for a drink. She'd missed all that as much as the love-making, the planning for their future, the big issues every couple faced. It had been a long time without someone close, someone of her own. If only this day could last for ever.

Really? Really.

At the top of Trafalgar Street they turned into a pub where tourists and locals leaned against the bar or sat around tables.

'What are you having?' she asked. 'Beer? And a late lunch?'

'Yes and yes.' He chose a local beer from the list on the blackboard. Then added, 'Seafood chowder for me.'

Seated in a corner, Nikki rested her elbows on the table and her chin in her hands. 'This is the life. I feel so removed from work, it's wonderful.'

Her gaze travelled over the patrons, finally pausing on a couple in their thirties. The woman nursed a wee baby wrapped in a blue blanket and sipped an orange juice while her husband enjoyed a lager. Nikki watched with a sense of longing that had recently begun expanding within her. What would it be like to hold your own child? To be a mum?

'You've gone all dreamy.' Fraser nudged her.

Oops. She shook away those thoughts. 'People watching.'

'The couple with the baby?' His eyes narrowed.

She tried for nonchalance. 'Well, he is cute.' She sipped her beer and didn't look at Fraser. 'At home everyone's excited about Beau and Yvonne's baby, even though it's not due until Christmas.'

'I bet they are.'

'Yvonne let me touch her tummy when the baby kicked. It was amazing. Made me realise that's a real person inside there.' When Fraser's eyebrows rose she grinned. 'Yeah, I know a baby's a real person, but feeling his kicks really brought it home to me how wonderful the whole process of having a baby really is.'

Fraser's jaw had dropped. She blushed and reached for her glass, taking a mouthful of beer to stop herself from saying anything else. But she'd been ecstatic after that moment, had even started wondering if she'd ever know the joy of motherhood.

'Their lives are going to change for ever.'

'Change in a good way, surely?' She blinked. Didn't Fraser want children? He must. He'd put sperm on ice, hadn't he?

'Sorry. Did I sound glum? It's this thing with Dad. You're so right, life goes round in circles.'

Absolutely. The past couple of days had brought it home to her in a way she'd never considered before. Her parents and brothers had always been there for her, supporting her, looking out for her, as she had for them in her own way. And now there'd be a new generation in her family. 'It's exciting.' Someone for her to take care of.

She'd driven back to the flat last night thinking about her future. Until now she'd truly believed that her work could satisfy her completely and that not getting married and having babies didn't matter. She'd been playing safe. Fraser's return had started her questioning everything in her life and feeling that tiny kick against the palm of her hand made her want more. A man to love, a baby in her arms and a house she could call home. The stuff that life was really about.

'Time to hit the road.' Fraser was watching her, looking as handsome as ever, as familiar and lovable as he always had. The man of her dreams?

As long as it wasn't the impossible dream.

Fraser smiled across at Nikki as her eyelids drooped. He spoke quietly so as not to wake her. 'Hey, sleepyhead, you're supposed to be chattering to me, keeping me alert as I drive.'

'Hmm.' Jerking her head up, she stared out the windscreen before shuffling her shoulders against the seat to get more comfortable. Her chin fell forward and her eyes closed again.

Warmth stole through him as he took quick glances at her. Nikki. Nik. She'd been there for him today. Not interfering or taking over with his dad, just there with a smile or a touch. As she had when his dad had gone missing last week. He liked it that she didn't made a song and dance about anything. He liked it that she felt she could stand by him. Maybe she was beginning to accept him again, to want to be with him in the rest of his life outside work.

He slowed for the first of many tight corners on the road going over the Whangamoa hills as they headed away from Nelson. And recalled the misty look in Nikki's eyes as she'd talked about Yvonne's baby. She wanted children of her own. That had been apparent as she'd kept glancing across at the tiny baby in blue. Would she be prepared to have them his way? In vitro.

He braked. 'Hell, man, look out.' The car in front weaved across the middle line, and Fraser drove even slower, keeping his distance.

Nikki stirred, lifted her head, peered around. 'What's going on?'

'The guy in front's driving very erratically. A moment ago he was half across the median.' Fraser gaped in astonishment. 'And now he's overcompensated and his wheels are in the loose gravel on the outside of the road.'

They both flinched as stones flicked back at them. Fraser held the horn down for a long moment. 'Come on, man. You shouldn't be on the road.'

'Hope he keeps to his side of the road when there's traffic coming the other way. Especially any freight trucks. That would be messy.' Nikki watched the saloon in front. 'Is he drunk?'

'Quite possibly.'

'Nothing we can do if he won't pull over,' Nik muttered. 'No cellphone coverage in these hills.'

Rounding a sharp bend, Fraser braked hard. Nikki jerked forward, gasping loudly. Ahead, the saloon scraped along the rocky bank and stopped abruptly.

'Are you all right?' Fraser asked Nikki as he flicked on the hazard lights.

'I'm fine. Got a fright, that's all.' She was already half out of the car. 'Let's check this guy out.'

When Fraser pulled the driver's door open, ready to give the man a blasting for his appalling driving, Nikki automatically bent to catch the man as he slid half out of his seat.

'Hey, careful, I've got you.' She spoke quietly, confidently.

Fraser took the man's weight and helped Nikki ease him back inside before turning the ignition off.

Then Nik opened the back door and clambered inside, squeezed between the seats to the front. 'Sir, are you all right?' Automatically, she reached for his wrist, feeling for a pulse. 'Sir, my name is Nikki and this is Fraser. We're both ambulance paramedics. Do you mind if we check you over?'

'My chest hurts.' The words were drawn out and slurred. His free hand tapped his chest in the vicinity of his heart. 'Here. And here.' His hand slid carelessly down his left arm.

His face was grey and sweaty. His pulse was too slow and he was struggling to breathe. She glanced at Fraser and shook her head. 'We need help,' she told him very quietly.

'Onto it. I'll stop the next car heading into Nelson and get them to call 111 the moment they get phone coverage.'

'There are houses at the bottom of the hill and a store another couple of kilometres along.'

Then Nikki returned her attention to the man, her lips moving as she started counting his respiration rate.

Fraser turned as another car pulled up, followed by a large truck and trailer unit. 'Yes, trucks have radios.' He crossed to the truck and asked, 'Can you call the emergency services?'

'Sure can, mate. What do you need?'

'Ambulance and traffic. One patient.' Fraser gave the bare details he had. 'That car's going to need towing too.' Then he returned to Nikki, who'd need his help if the driver was really ill. From the sound of loud voices someone had started to sort out the traffic snarl already developing.

Poking his head inside the car, he told Nikki, 'A truckie's calling up on his radio so that should speed things up a bit. What have we got here?'

Nikki glanced up. 'This is Roy Constable, and he's been feeling unwell for a while.' Looking back at her patient, she added, 'Resp rate is down.'

As Fraser watched he saw Roy gasping as though he wasn't getting enough oxygen. If only they had a tank with them.

Roy spoke slowly between gasps. 'I felt crook. Before I left my daughter's in Nelson. Thought it was indigestion.'

Fraser squeezed Roy's shoulder. 'Have you ever had anything like this before?' Indigestion and heart attacks were often mixed up, the pain initially similar.

'Not really.' He winced. 'Ahh. It's getting worse.' His lips quivered as he tried to suck in a lungful of air. 'I wanted to get home.'

Silly man. Why hadn't he pulled over? He was extremely lucky not to have had an accident involving another vehicle. But it wasn't his place to point that out. 'Where's home?'

'Rai Valley.'

Great. A few houses, one café, a petrol station and a farming supplies store. No doctor. No ambulance. No help. 'Okay, Roy, I want you to stay still and try to relax. We're getting an ambulance to come out for you.' But that was going to take forty-five minutes at least, he calculated. Hopefully Roy wouldn't work it out. That would definitely increase his anxiety level. Fingers crossed, Roy didn't have a full-blown cardiac arrest before the arrival of a fully equipped truck. But if he did then he and Nikki would be able to start CPR immediately.

Nikki sat back. There was nothing for her to do but keep an eye on Roy and wait for help to arrive. 'What were the odds of us being right behind the guy when he crashed?'

Fraser grimaced. 'What were the odds he'd slide into the bank and not go over the edge on the other side?'

Roy's eyes were closed, and his respiration rate had slowed further.

A screech of tyres made Nikki jump. 'Idiot,' she muttered. 'We need a traffic cop here before we're dealing with more patients.'

Roy groaned long and loud, his hands grasping at air. Nikki took his wrist and began counting his pulse again.

At least he still had one, Fraser thought as he straightened up. 'I wonder what's in the back of his car that we could lay him on if we have to.' He reached in and popped the boot before disappearing round the back to take a look. 'Nothing.'

He returned to hunker down by the car and talked quietly as they waited for the ambulance to arrive. 'Days like these I'm glad I'm medically trained.'

The *whoo-whoo* of a siren screeched through the air. 'That was quick.' Nikki glanced along the road to the corner but Fraser saw her hope fade as the familiar white car with yellow and blue strips pulled up. 'Not the ambulance, then.'

The traffic cop who got out of the car shoved his hat on his head and strode across to them. 'The ambulance is about five minutes behind me. What happened?'

Fraser quickly filled him in on details of the accident. Within moments the cop was directing the traffic one way at a time on the narrow road.

When the ambulance pulled up Nikki made the handover while Fraser helped extricate Roy from his car onto the stretcher.

'Let's try for home again.' Fraser draped an arm over Nikki's shoulders and turned her towards their vehicle. 'Blenheim, here we come. I hope.'

Under his arm Nik twisted to look at him. 'We make a great team.' She raised one hand, high-fived him. 'We both knew what to do without having to spell it out. Awesome.'

Awesome. *So are you, my girl.* Who'd have believed the excellent chef he'd once known would turn out to be such a good paramedic? Especially when the sight of blood used to turn her white and giddy. She never ceased to surprise him.

He held the passenger door open for her. As she ducked around him he smelt peonies and smiled. That scent had been made for her. Evocative, sensual, very feminine. Nik.

He'd better get into the car and drive before he took her in his arms and held her for ever. Shutting her door, he strode around the car and slipped inside.

Nikki sighed. 'So much for a day off. It's like a busman's holiday.'

Fraser turned the engine over, at the same time jerking his thumb towards the back seat. 'I don't think those bags have anything to do with being an AP but all to do with looking gorgeous when you're not in your uniform.'

'Take me home, then. I've got a lot of unpacking and putting away to do.' She grinned, more relaxed with him than he'd seen her in the past couple of months.

'Yes, ma'am.' Fraser grinned back before

slowly easing between two cars in preparation for heading on up the hill. Three steps forward. None back? Again. Progress was being made. His grin stretched wider.

CHAPTER TEN

FRASER watched Nikki from under half-lowered eyelids as she read a magazine. Except she hadn't turned a single page in the past twenty minutes. So far their shift had been very quiet for a Friday night. Too quiet. Without work to focus on, his brain was running riot with images of Nikki.

Nikki driving the ambulance.

Nikki holding that guy in his car on the Whangamoas.

Nikki burning the scrambled eggs, and another time walking in here with enough chocolate brownies to feed half the town.

Nikki in his arms, kissing him.

His chair crashed against the wall as he stood up. Damn it, he needed some air. He pushed out through the main door into the parking area and dragged in a lungful of warm evening air. Thank goodness for spring when there was no need for heavy jackets or jerseys.

He needed to get away from her. She'd gone back to being a work colleague and nothing else since their day in Nelson, which was starting to irritate him. It was as though she regretted the kisses they'd shared, and the love-making. As if she had more issues to clear up but wasn't outright asking him about them. If they were even about him. He suspected they were. So why couldn't she say what was on her mind? She'd harped on about not believing he had returned permanently, mentioned on more than one occasion that he should return to his medical studies. What did she want from him?

Hands on hips, he leaned back and stared up into the clear night sky filled with stars. Three steps back. Talk about being all over the place.

At least his mum and dad were back home after the endless rounds of discussions with doctors, specialists and rest-home managers. His mum had finally conceded it was time to let his dad go into care, but it was breaking her heart to do it, so he'd made a point of being at home every moment he wasn't here.

With one exception. The day he'd visited the Page clan. He'd planned on seeing Allan and Rose before tracking down Jay and Beau, but when he'd turned up at the homestead everyone had been there. Including Nikki. His heartfelt thanks for what they'd done in helping to find his dad had been well received. Like old times. Once again he was completely at home in the Page house. It felt good, great.

Even Nikki hadn't been as distant as she was at work. Probably secure with her brothers all over the place, minding her business for her.

The way she'd stayed with him when he'd learned his dad was missing had got to him, reminded him again how badly he'd treated her all that time ago. Nik had not backed off from a potential problem, supporting him instead of leaving him to his own resources. Gawd, he loved her. But until she learned to trust him again he wouldn't make any headway. Only time was going to show her he meant everything he had said.

In the office the radio squawked at the same moment his pager vibrated on his hip. At last.

Locking the door, he hurried to the ambulance, unhooked the power supply and climbed inside.

Nikki slid into the driver's seat. 'What's the address?'

'Holdsworth Road. Know it?' Fraser read the screen.

'Yes.'

'Asthmatic with chest pains. Sixty-nine-year-old man.'

'Who?'

'David White. The head of science at the boys' college was a David White. The age seems about right.'

'Could be the same man, then.'

A neighbour let them into the house. 'I came over when I saw the lights still on. He's never up after ten and it's now gone midnight. He's struggling to breathe.'

Fraser placed the pack on the lounge floor and knelt down beside his old teacher, the man who'd inspired him to keep following his dream. 'Hello, sir. Got yourself in a spot of bother, have you?'

'Fraser…' David tried to inhale. 'Is that you?' he gasped.

'Yes, it is. Bet you never thought I'd be turning up to help you out. Have you taken any asthma meds in the past hour?' Fraser was taking obs as he talked.

David moved his head sideways. 'No,' he mouthed. Then his eyes widened. 'Nikki? With you.' David wheezed. 'Good. Back together.'

'Only working together,' Nikki was quick to reply as she prepared the nebuliser to administer salbutamol.

'I'm going to give you a shot of adrenaline, David.'

David nodded once. 'Getting worse,' he squeezed out.

Fraser rapidly rechecked his patient's obs. 'Slipping in and out of consciousness. I'll set up an IV port ready for more adrenaline if he goes under.'

Nikki nodded. 'Wait twenty minutes before a second dose if you can.'

'Will do.'

'As soon as you're done we'll get him on the stretcher and loaded up.'

Fraser drove away from ED after they'd handed

their patient over to the night staff. 'I wonder why David let his attack get so bad?'

'Didn't want to be a nuisance?' Nikki mused. 'We get plenty of those.'

'I wouldn't have thought he'd be like that. He's severely compromised himself now.'

She'd seen how it had upset Fraser to see his old teacher in such a state. 'The nurses in ED will give him a lecture, believe me. I've heard them do that on more than one occasion.' Nikki stretched her legs as much as possible in the confines of the cab. Her stomach rumbled—loudly. She grinned. 'Can we go by a burger bar?'

'Anything to stop that racket.'

'Cancel the burger.' Nikki reached for the handset. 'Blenheim One, go ahead.'

The coms operator's voice crackled loudly in the truck. 'Priority-one call. Male, eighteen years, Eugene Clark, heavy blood loss from right arm. Be aware, possible stabbing, police have been notified.'

'Roger, Coms. And thanks.' Nikki grimaced. 'It's one-thirty in the morning. We've got to be dealing with drunks.'

'Possibly.'

She hadn't finished. 'I just love stabbings. Everyone will be off their heads with booze and drugs. They'll be angry and looking for another fight. The patient will be belligerent and swearing fit to bust. And us? We'll be trying to be nice and helpful.'

Fraser winced. 'Sounds like a heap of fun.'

She watched Fraser as he sped through the dark, empty streets, ever watchful of the road and looking out for walking partygoers thinking they had the street to themselves. Hopefully the flashing lights were enough to warn anyone out and about of their presence. At this time of night the siren was a last resort.

Nikki nibbled her top lip, feeling more uneasy than usual. 'Remember the first priority is our own safety. If the crowd looks dangerous, we wait for police back-up or leave.'

'Gotcha.' He indicated a left turn. 'I've been to these sorts of situations before, Nik. Often.' He reached across, gently squeezed her thigh. 'We'll be careful.'

'Sure.' Of course they would. But she had a bad feeling about this one.

'Here we go.'

Nikki peered through the dark. 'That's one hell of a crowd. All young men, by the look of it. I hope they're not going to give us any grief.'

A policeman opened her door. 'Hey, Nikki, how're you doing?'

Relief loosened the tension gripping her. Thank goodness for the boys in blue. They weren't quite so alone now. 'Just fine, Grant. What's the mood here?' Nikki slid to the ground.

'Tense, but they'll leave you alone, I think. We'll be watching your backs.' Grant nodded at a line of three of his colleagues. 'The victim's behind our men.'

Slinging her pack on her back, Nikki closed the back door firmly. 'Can someone keep an eye on our truck?'

Grant said, 'Absolutely.'

Keeping close to Fraser, she pushed through the jostling young men. After one crude remark Fraser took her elbow and whispered, 'Ignore them.'

'I am,' she replied, but the shiver rolling through her body undermined her conviction. The atmosphere heaved with loud rock music and something else. Something she couldn't put her finger on. It worried her. One wrong move from any of these guys and she was leaving. Ambulance crews were told time and again not to put themselves in any danger.

And tonight things felt dangerous.

Then they were looking down at their patient and she pushed her concerns aside.

Eugene lay sprawled on the pavement, his arm bound tightly with a towel in an attempt to slow the heavy bleeding. It wasn't doing the job. He was groaning and cursing everyone in sight, especially the police. Patches of vomit were mixed with the massive pool of blood next to the lad's body.

Nikki knelt beside him. 'Eugene, my name's Nikki and this is Fraser. We're paramedics from the ambulance service. I need to look at your arm.'

She reared back at the expletives that spewed from Eugene's mouth, her shoulder slamming into Fraser's knees and knocking him off balance. 'Sorry,' she muttered when he crouched down beside her.

Leaning forward, he said as calmly as he could manage, 'Listen, we're here to help you so stop carrying on like that and let us get on with it. The sooner we're done the sooner we can get you to hospital and out of pain.'

Following Fraser's example, Nikki drew a deep breath to calm her thumping heart and looked around the immediate area then back at their patient. 'By the amount of blood covering the pavement, Eugene's in serious risk of going into shock and organ failure,' she said quietly.

'Aren't you going to give me some drugs now?' Eugene's eyes widened. 'I'm hurting real bad.'

'I'm sure you are. We'll give you some gas in a minute, but we also need to stop the bleeding.' Fraser had a face mask ready.

Nikki reached into the bag for some scissors and asked quietly, 'Want to tell me what happened?'

'What's that got to do with you, cow? Just fix me up.'

Beside her Fraser drew an angry breath then stood to ask the cops if they knew what had happened. When he returned to crouching beside Nikki he told her, 'Knife wound. Grant put this towel in place before being edged away by some of Eugene's mates.' He reached for the lad's good arm, wrapped a cuff around it. 'Eugene, I'm going to take your blood pressure. Can you stay still for a moment?'

Nikki murmured, 'Unfortunately that towel isn't stopping the bleeding. I'm going to have to risk removing it to put a tourniquet on.' She began snipping at the soaked towel.

'Hey, lady, what are you doing? You can't take that off his arm. You'll kill him.' A young man, bouncing from one foot to the other, loomed up on her other side, anger glaring out at her from his mean-looking eyes. Then he stuck his fingers in his mouth and let loose with a piercing whistle.

She shivered, glanced behind, heard shouting break out on the opposite side of the crowd. The cops took off, heading for the fracas. Three menacingly silent youths slid in beside Nikki and Fraser.

Her tongue moistened her lips. 'We're helping your friend.' If Eugene wasn't their friend, she and Fraser were in trouble.

The biggest and meanest of the trio grabbed Nikki's shoulder, his fingers digging in so hard the knuckles were white. 'You think we're stupid? You're gonna make him bleed to death.'

'Hey.' Fraser spun on his feet. 'Let her go, mate. She's trying to save Eugene's life.' Anger glittered from his eyes.

Light glinted on the wide blade of a knife in her assailant's hand. 'Not if she takes that towel off she's not. I know you have to put pressure on a cut to stop the bleeding.' His fingers dug deeper and he carved a pattern in the air right before her face.

Nikki could feel her knees knocking. The air in her lungs caught. Her skin went icy. What could she say to deflate this madman's attitude? Her mind was blank.

Fraser stepped closer, glared into the man's face. 'Let her go or your pal isn't going to get any help.'

'That so?' The young man splayed his legs, waving the knife between them. He jerked a thumb at Nikki. 'She your woman?'

Fraser didn't hesitate. 'Yeah, man, she is.'

I am? Did he mean it? Or was he just saying it to defuse the situation? She tried moving her shoulder free.

The guy gripped harder, spun her round. 'Let's show him what it's like when his woman's hurt.' And the hand holding the knife rose, the blade flashing in the light.

Nikki watched, breathless, with her feet rooted to the ground, appalled as the blade descended, fast, aimed directly at her. Then she was shoved sideways, slamming onto the road. Her elbow cracked hard, pain ricocheting up and down her arm. Her hip thumped hard, more pain hitting her, winding her.

Then something, someone, toppled, fell over her feet. 'Fraser,' she screamed. And scrambled to get clear and reach for him.

The knife handle protruded from the side of Fraser's chest. Nausea roiled up her throat. She swallowed hard. *Don't be sick now.* Fraser needed her. What to do? Her brain was not functioning. Remove the knife? Wrong. Load him and drive like hell for the hospital? Made more sense than anything else. She needed help getting him to the ambulance.

'Fraser, talk to me,' she pleaded, and looked at his face. Blood pumped from a head wound, tracking over his forehead, down his cheek.

When she touched him, his head lolled sideways. He was unconscious. Had his head hit the tarmac?

'Hey, Nikki, move over, girl. We're here now. We'll take care of Fraser.'

She blinked, took a quick sideways glance. 'Mike? Rebecca?'

'We heard on the radio there was a problem here so thought you could do with some support.' Mike already had Fraser's shirt cut away from the wound.

Nikki wobbled on her haunches as she gripped Fraser's hand. 'Hang in there, Fraser, love.' She knew she sounded desperate. She didn't care. 'You have to save him, Mike.'

'We will. I promise.' He gave her a quick hug. 'Now, move a bit so I can get to your man.'

The second person to have called Fraser her man. Maybe they were right, and she should just get over the past. Completely. She blinked and looked around. 'Where is everyone? What happened to the crowd?' Strength had returned to her voice now that Mike and Rebecca were here and she wasn't dealing with this alone.

'Disappeared in a flaming hurry, from what

Grant told us. No one's sticking around to take the rap for this.' Rebecca knelt on the other side of Fraser, calmly working on him.

Tears pricked Nikki's eyelids and streaked down her cheeks. 'Thanks, guys. I lost it. I didn't know what to do.' Her thumb stroked Fraser's hand without stopping, willing him to be all right. How? He had a ruddy great knife sticking out from between his ribs. She knew all the implications of that. She shivered as her skin chilled.

'Who would remember anything in these circumstances?' Rebecca smiled.

Mike turned to Nikki. 'I know you don't want to leave Fraser's side but could you ask Grant and his colleagues to load the other patient and drive him to the ED?'

She didn't want to. 'Okay.' Letting go of Fraser's hand was difficult, peeling one finger back at a time. But Mike was right. Eugene was entitled to be helped, regardless of what his mate had done to the man she cared for most in this world. But before she stood up she placed the softest of kisses on Fraser's cold lips. 'Hang in there. You and I are not finished yet.'

CHAPTER ELEVEN

NIKKI curled up uncomfortably on a chair beside Fraser's bed. The beeping of the machines monitoring his breathing reassured her. Something had to tell her. Fraser wasn't. He lay so still. Too still. Nothing like his usual active self.

His hand lay in hers, not reacting to any of her light squeezing. Bruises covered his forehead and his left cheek was swollen. A shaved patch on his head showed a wound stitched together. According to the surgeon, Fraser had been very lucky. A concussion but no lasting damage to the brain.

Add to that a punctured lung and one nicked rib, and he was lucky?

Her bottom lip quivered. He *was* lucky. He could've been killed. 'He saved my life.'

On the opposite side of the bed Molly smiled wearily. 'Don't go blaming yourself. Fraser would never let anything happen to you if he could help it.'

'Aren't you angry at him for leaping between me and that knife? At me because he cared enough to do that?' Dang, *she* was angry. Fraser should not be lying here. She should. It was her that guy had wanted to hurt. Not Fraser.

'The only person I'm angry at is the man who did this. I know I sound old when I say it wouldn't have happened when we were your age.'

Nikki couldn't stop the chuckle that rolled off her tongue. 'Remind me not to say that when my kids are getting into trouble.' She squeezed Fraser's hand and looked at his mother. 'Thanks, Molly, you've cheered me up.'

Molly pushed off her chair. 'I'd better go and see Ken. He'll be fretting because I'm late.'

'What are you going to tell him about this?'

'I doubt I'll say a word. It will only distress him when there's nothing he can do about it.'

'But you must tell him. Ken has a right to know, surely? Wouldn't you want to know? I would, if it was me.' Like mother, like son? Had

Molly always kept things from Ken, or was her reaction due to his illness?

'Molly flushed. 'I'm protecting Ken, saving him added stress. Stress only makes him so much worse. And I don't want that.'

Placing Fraser's hand on the bedcover, Nikki went to his mother and embraced her. 'I should mind my own business. You're right. Ken's already got enough problems.' She leaned back and looked into Molly's sad eyes. 'So have you. Anything I can do to help, make sure you ring and tell me. Okay?' She shook this lovely woman gently. 'I mean that.'

Molly looked down at her son. 'You're already doing lots.' And then she was gone, leaving Nikki to puzzle the meaning of her words.

'Hey, sis, how's he doing?' Jay strode into the room and engulfed her in a bear hug. 'You okay?'

Sniff, sniff. 'Couldn't be better. And Fraser's going to be all right.' Dang, she hadn't cried all night and now with Jay holding her, concern in his voice for her and Fraser, it was as though someone had opened the floodgates.

'Now, what did I do to deserve this?' Jay

pushed her down into the chair and reached for a box of tissues. 'Here, use these,' he said gruffly, 'then tell me all the details. I hear the cops arrested the guy who stabbed Fraser.'

Her eyes widened, spilling more tears down her face. 'They have? Good.' Nikki filled Jay in on everything. 'Fraser was protecting me, Jay.'

'I'd be stunned if he hadn't.'

Her gaze returned to Fraser. 'Yeah, you're right. He'd never let anyone hurt me.' Funny thing, that.

Fraser tried to stretch but stopped as pain stabbed his chest. Gingerly lifting his eyelids, he peered out at the white room, the metal bedrails. Hospital. That explained the pain. Sort of. Turning his head to one side, he bit down on an oath as a bomb went off inside his head. Lights flashed in front of his eyes.

What had happened to him? Was he all right? As in not seriously injured?

Closing his eyes, he concentrated on his body. Wriggled his toes. No problem there. Stretched his calves. Good. Lifted his left arm, and sucked air through his clenched teeth. That cranked up the dull throbbing in his chest, making him want to stop breathing for a while till everything settled down again. His right arm felt heavy, weighed down.

He popped his eyes open, turned his head slowly to avoid another explosion, and stopped. His whole body softened, warmed. Nik. Beautiful Nik. Sitting on a chair, leaning so her top half was sprawled on the bed, she slept. Her head lay against his arm, her breathing warm on his skin.

And then he remembered. The knife. Aimed at Nikki. Going for her. His frantic leap. Then the hot pain as the blade had slammed into him.

Thank goodness. Or it would be Nikki lying here. Or worse.

Carefully, so as not to wake her, he shifted his arm and placed his hand on her head. Threaded his fingers through her messy hair, feeling the silky tangles on his skin. He closed his eyes again. Drank in the sweetness of the moment. He and Nik. Together. However temporarily.

'Nikki, there's something I have to tell you.' Fraser sat up in bed, the robe he wore revealing more chest than was good for her heart rate.

'You sound serious.' Hadn't they had enough serious stuff to last a lifetime? Two days after the stabbing and the police had finally stopped calling in with questions, their colleagues had found their smiles, and her brothers had stopped suggesting she go back to cooking for a career.

'I need you to trust me, believe I'll never deliberately hurt you, so there is one more thing you should know about why I called off the wedding.'

Nikki leaned close, kissed those seductive lips that weren't smiling. Running her forefinger along his jaw, she asked, 'Do you think I care about that any more? I love you, and that's all that matters.'

His eyes widened in surprise. So did hers. She felt her eyebrows lifting. When had she come to that conclusion? Some time during the long night waiting for Fraser to come out of surgery, to regain consciousness. But talk about springing it on him, on her. Shouldn't she have taken her time to get used to the idea first?

'Say that again,' he whispered. 'The bit about loving me.'

She wasn't taking it back. 'I love you.'

He caught her hand, kissed each fingertip. Then he reached for her, slipping his arms around her in the gentlest of hugs.

Her badly bruised elbow ached as it rubbed against his thigh, but she daren't move it for fear of knocking the drain in Fraser's chest wound. Instead, she lifted her mouth to his, glad of the distraction for both of them. Then the kiss took over and she was lost in the heat of Fraser's mouth claiming hers. A breathless kiss due to Fraser's pierced lung. But a kiss nonetheless.

'You won't be wanting a cup of tea, then,' an aide called from the doorway.

They jerked apart, Fraser gasping at the sudden movement. 'Not at the moment,' he finally managed to mutter.

When the woman had taken her broad smile and the tea trolley away Fraser grinned. 'How could I drink tea after kissing you?' Then his mouth straightened. 'You distracted me. But I haven't forgotten what I was going to tell you.'

Nikki shifted uneasily at the serious look in his eyes. He loved her, right? She hadn't exposed her heart to have him tell her they weren't ever getting back together. 'Dang. Do you have to?'

'Yes, Nik, I do. Because, my lovely, despite what you say, you still don't believe my reasons for not telling you about the cancer were justified. And you're right. I probably would've told you right from the get-go if not for one thing. I truly wanted you with me, desperately needed your strength, right from the start. Every time I thought I could tell you, only one thing made me stay away. And staying away was as hard as dealing with the news, believe me.'

Her heart slowed, almost stopped. This was not working out how she'd hoped. This did not sound like a declaration of his love for her. She leaned back so she could see every emotion that crossed his face, wanting to see exactly how he felt as he talked. 'Go on.'

His chest lifted, and he opened his mouth. 'My oncologist was so truthful it was gutting. He warned that after the surgery there was a likelihood that I'd be impotent.'

Nikki gasped, pressed the fingers of one hand to her mouth. She stared at him, stunned. 'Oh, my God.' Reaching with her free hand, she cupped his cheek.

'That's why I stayed away.' He turned his

mouth to kiss first her thumb, then each finger, then put her hand away from him. Stared deeply into her eyes. 'Now do you understand? Can you see why I couldn't tell you?'

She swallowed. Nodded. Tears welled. For him? For them? Finally, she whispered, 'I still wish you had told me, but I understand why you felt you couldn't. What an impossible situation.'

'It was.'

'We could've put the wedding on hold.'

'You really think so? The tension between us would've been horrendous.' He flinched. 'Hell, when the time came I probably wouldn't have been able to perform anyway, I'd have been beyond nervous. There'd have been far too much riding on the outcome.'

'You were doomed if you did, doomed if you didn't. But don't you see how disappearing with hardly a word was so painful for me? How it nearly destroyed both of us?' Fraser winced. 'You shut me out. You didn't give me a chance to choose, you just decided for me.'

'I know, and I'm sorry. I'm sorry for everything I put you through. I wasn't exactly coping very well at the time. I wanted to save you from having to make that decision, from living with your choice.' He looked up into her eyes. 'Please believe me when I say that I was trying to protect you.'

Nikki laced her fingers on her lap. She stared at her manicured nails, remembering another time she'd had them done. Light pink to match her wedding bouquet of peonies. She'd never worn anything remotely pink since.

She shivered. Impotent. Fraser? Impossible. It would've destroyed him. She understood the difficult situation he had been in, and why he had struggled to tell her the truth. How could a man tell anyone that, least of all the woman he was about to marry? Raising her head, she said in an unsteady voice, 'I'm glad you're okay.' Then she blushed crimson. 'I mean, in all respects, the cancer, everything,' she blustered.

'I'm glad, too. Very glad.' His gaze was fixed on her. Watching every nuance on her face? He added, 'More than glad. In all respects.'

'Spoken like a man.'

He smiled, a deep smile that warmed her through, that teased and promised so much. 'How else would you have me say it?'

She couldn't answer.

'Nik,' he said softly, 'I never stopped loving you, not for one moment. There were times, I swear, I wouldn't have got through it if I hadn't carried a picture of you in my head. All those wonderful memories we created gave me the strength to fight, made me realise how much I had to live for.'

'Really?' she croaked. Clearing her throat, she tried again. 'You mean that?'

'I understand your disbelief but, yes, sweetheart, I love you. Always have, always will.'

Her lips were trembling when she placed them on his mouth. Her hands shook as she held his shoulders, her body soft against his. 'You love me.'

She tasted so sweet. So Nik. So much his life. Stirring him, heating his blood in a slow, loving way, making him long to be joined with her.

'Huh-hum.'

The second interruption of the afternoon. 'Can't a man get any peace in here?'

His surgeon shook his head in amusement. 'Anyone point out that you're in hospital? You know, where sick people go?'

'Every minute of the day.' Fraser grinned and let Nikki sit up. Her face was scarlet as she crossed to sit on the chair.

But as Fraser discussed his wound and treatment with the surgeon he was very aware that Nikki's gaze never left him, and that the sparkle produced when he'd told her he loved her was slowly evaporating.

Fraser woke late in the afternoon to the sound of someone moaning in the next bed. Sleeping in hospital wasn't the greatest. Usually the moment he nodded off someone came along and prodded him or took his temperature or lifted the sheet to see his wound, which had become infected.

'The guy could've at least cleaned the blade before sticking it into me.'

'Be thankful the first man he used it on didn't have hepatitis A or something equally nice,' Jay drawled from by the window.

'How long have you been here?' One member or another of Nikki's family was always dropping in. 'Where's Nikki?'

'Long enough to know you talk in your sleep but not long enough to hear anything juicy. And

Nikki said she had to go see Mike about starting back at work.' Jay sat on the end of the bed. 'Any more questions?'

'The vet clinic not doing very well at the moment?' Fraser asked. Apart from Nikki, Jay was his most frequent visitor. He didn't believe Nikki had gone to see Mike. There'd been a strange look in her eyes when the surgeon had been with him. Wait till he saw her next. He'd dig for some answers.

'Flat out, actually. I don't know why people think their dogs and cats should partake in the pre-Christmas nibbles. We're seeing so many pets with tummy trouble, it's not funny.'

'Not a lot different to our job, then.'

'Anyone told you when you're getting out of here?' Jay asked.

'Hopefully tomorrow. But I'm on sick leave for at least another week. They won't even allow me to work in the office. Probably not stupid. Paperwork is definitely not my forte.'

'You'll have plenty to do at home. According to Mum, Molly's getting stuck into clearing out the house. You mightn't have a bed by tomorrow.'

Fraser swallowed the flare of annoyance. 'I wish she'd waited. That's not a job to do alone. But it's like she's decided to make a completely new start and doesn't want to waste any time moving into the townhouse she's bought near the retirement village.'

'If you think she's doing this on her own, you don't know the Page women. Mum and Nikki are with her. And Dad's been taking trailer loads of furniture to the second-hand gear shop and a whole heap of other stuff to the tip.'

'I'm glad Rose and Nikki are helping.' His hands curled into fists. 'It should've been me, though.'

Jay stood up. 'Time I went. But for the record you can't be there for everyone and if I had a choice I'm glad it was Nikki you were there for the other night.'

He shuddered. 'Me, too.'

He watched Jay saunter out of the room and gave a thankful sigh. He'd come a full circle, back on side with Nikki and her family. Definitely getting ahead now.

And Nikki loved him. How lucky could he

get? As soon as he was up and about he had plans of his own to get under way.

Nikki sauntered into his room that evening, a covered plate containing chicken enchilada in one hand, two take-out coffees in the other. 'Thought you'd like some real food for a change.'

'What I'd really like is to go home and keep an eye on what Mum's throwing out.'

'Who's a grumpy boy, then?' Nikki popped the top of one coffee and blew on the liquid. 'What's bugging you?'

'List everything that's gone to the tip. I bet there are things that I'd like to keep.'

'I doubt it. Old and broken shovel handles, rusty saws, a chainsaw that had to be the first ever produced. A thousand bent nails. Blown light bulbs. Why did Ken keep all that anyway?'

'He's always been a hoarder.' Fraser took a bite of his supper. And some of the tension gripping him since Jay's visit receded. 'This is wonderful. I don't suppose you sneaked a beer in to go with it.'

The way her eyes rolled told him she hadn't.

'You're not like your dad, are you? You won't spend your life filling sheds with junk?'

No, I'm going to spend it filling my house with a wife and kids. 'Not likely.'

'Thank goodness.' She pulled the chair across to the window and sat down, nursing her coffee. A frown creased her forehead. The same frown that had been there when she'd left after their discussion about his possible impotency.

He'd thought they'd finally gone through everything they needed to so they could move on. 'What's up?'

Her head twisted at an angle as she looked at him through her long eyelashes. Her mouth was tight, not unfriendly, not overly loving either. He couldn't read her. Her hand was steady when she raised the paper cup to her lips.

'Nik?' His heart started thudding. Was she about to retract her love? He couldn't bear that. Anything but that.

Those blue eyes focused directly on him, boring into him. 'When you decide to go back to med school, I'll help you.'

When he opened his mouth to deny her words she held her hand up. 'Spare me your denial.

I've seen in your eyes the hunger to be a part of the medical system whenever we've brought a patient into ED.' She sipped her coffee. 'You're meant to be a doctor. You want to be one. Going away to med school to finish your degree isn't going back on your word about staying here. The moment you qualify you'll be on the first plane home. Follow your dream, Fraser. Isn't that why you fought so hard for your life?' Tears glittered in her eyes.

They, more than her words, moved him. Did she think she was letting him go? Freeing him? He stared at her in wonder. She loved him and yet she was telling him to do what he hankered after. 'I promised you I'd stay. And Mum. She needs me.'

'Molly is moving into a low-maintenance property that she can manage easily. Anyway, there are enough men in my family to take care of any problems. And if you went to Wellington you'd only be twenty-five minutes away by air.' She drained her coffee and scrunched the cup tight. 'And if you need funds to get through, I've got money put aside. Grandma left me a healthy amount in her will.'

'I bet that's for your cake shop.' He wasn't taking that. 'You can't give away your dream for mine.'

'The cake shop idea is years away from happening, and by then you'll have paid me back.' Standing up, she tossed the cup into the bin and headed for the door. 'Think about it, Fraser. You know I'm right.'

CHAPTER TWELVE

'HEY, Mum, what's all this stuff?' Nikki asked as she surveyed the piles of cartons in the spare bedroom. It was Christmas Eve and Fraser's parents were coming to stay for the next two nights. With all her family around to keep an eye on Ken it hadn't been difficult to persuade Molly or his caregivers of the idea. 'It would take until Easter to clear this room.'

Her mother appeared at her side and reached for the door, pulling it shut. 'Just some things I've been collecting lately at the second-hand shops. I'll show you after Christmas once everyone's gone.'

'Second-hand what? Clothes? Cups and saucers?' This was so unlike her mother, a woman who lived by the adage that if you hadn't used or worn something in the past year then you no longer needed it, and off to a charity shop it went. 'And that many boxes? You're not starting your own shop, are you?'

'When would I have time for that? With my grandchild due to arrive any day, I'll hardly have time to get my gardening done.'

There was another thing. 'What's going on, Mum? I've never see the gardens looking so wonderful. The roses are amazing. And I'm taking an armful of those pink and white peonies home with me at the end of the weekend.'

'I'm sure there's plenty out there so I won't notice some missing.' Her mother headed down the hall towards the kitchen. 'Now, come and help me polish the glasses for tomorrow. And don't worry about Molly and Ken. I'm putting them in Jay's old room.'

Perplexed, Nikki studied her mother. Why was her mum talking so fast, jabbering on about anything as though trying to sidetrack her? Aha, her mum had ducked the question about what was going on. Why? 'Here, use this.' A polishing cloth was pressed into her hands.

In the kitchen, Nikki delved into the back of the large walk-in pantry for the boxes of wine glasses and champagne flutes. 'What's this?'

She spied a box right at the back she'd never seen before and carefully tugged it out.

Her mother was immediately at her side, reaching for the box. 'Oh, just a couple of glasses I bought the other day.' She put the box back where Nikki had got it from. 'We're not using those tomorrow.'

Nikki turned to stare at this woman she'd known all her life. 'You still look like my mother.'

Red spilled through Rose's cheeks. 'I am your mother.'

'Really? I'm not so sure.' Nikki shook her head. This was getting way too weird. But right now there was a lot to do before tomorrow's festivities. Maybe by the time they had everything ready her real mother would be back and this stranger would've caught the bus out of town.

Then suddenly she was enveloped in her mother's arms, hugged fiercely. 'I'm very proud of you. You're special. My girl.'

Nikki hugged her back, blinking rapidly. Weirder and weirder.

'Merry Christmas.' Fraser walked up to Nikki and kissed her on both cheeks when he and his parents arrived at the Page farm early Christmas morning. Then he kissed her on the mouth, softly. His stomach squeezed with nerves. What if this didn't work out? What if she threw him off the farm? He felt a hand on his back. Not Nikki's. Her father's. Suddenly, he knew deep down inside that everything would work out just fine.

'Merry ho-ho to you too,' Nikki murmured against his mouth before turning to Molly and Ken. 'Merry Christmas to you both.'

His mum enveloped her in a hug. 'This is special, being here with your family. Thank you for inviting Ken. I know he's become a handful.'

Nikki gave his mother one of her heart-stopping smiles. 'We don't ignore people once something happens to them.'

His mother blinked and smiled back. Fraser knew she'd just been given the best present of the day. Unconditional acceptance of her beloved husband.

He caught Nikki's hand, drew her back to him. 'You look absolutely stunning.' Dressed in a clinging red dress that barely reached mid-thigh and a wide silver belt that accentuated her tiny waist, balancing on red shoes with impossible heels, she looked perfect. Good enough to eat. The Santa hat perched cheekily on her flowing hair brought a mist to his eyes. He loved Nikki more than he'd thought possible.

The scent of peonies wafted through the air. Peonies, bright and colourful, fragile and silky, the perfect perfume for Nikki. He watched as his father hugged this woman who'd shown him so much care and compassion, even love, over the past few months. Both his parents adored her. Even his dad—who had fewer and fewer lucid moments as the weeks progressed, hurtling towards a total fog and a shadow of the hulking man he'd once been—fully understood how special Nikki was. Her whole family had taken his small one in, making them welcome and a part of them.

Like today. It was Christmas Day on a grand scale with the McCalls. People everywhere. Nikki's parents, her brothers and their wives or partners, the partners' parents, and Amber, who was on duty on Boxing Day so she couldn't go down south to share the day with her folks.

Later in the day, Allan and Rose would open their home to all the local strays and waifs—as

Nikki called the neighbours who had nowhere to go or no one to share Christmas with—for a dinner that had to be seen to be believed, going by what Nikki had told him. Even Morag and Bryne had been invited to come along later in the morning.

Morag now worked on the farm and, along with Bryne, lived in one of the farm cottages. Another happy ending for someone Allan and Rose hadn't known until an accident had brought them all together.

'Good, I'm glad you've arrived.' Rose bounced down the steps. 'Now we really can get Christmas under way.'

'It's only eight o'clock.' Allan clasped Fraser's mum in a hug. 'I swear this is Rose's favourite day of the year. She's like a big kid, waiting for the presents to be opened.'

'Yes, well, we're all waiting for that today.' Fraser heard his mum say.

Fraser's breath caught in his throat. He'd hardly slept a wink last night waiting for the sun to come up. He'd have come around at five if he'd thought Nikki might be awake. Anything to get the gift giving out of the way. He couldn't believe how nervous he felt. Terrified even. What if—? *Quit the what-ifs. What would be would be.* He was done with doubts about the future. He knew what he wanted and he aimed to get it.

Thankfully, Jay thrust a glass of champagne into his shaking hand. 'Here you go, pal. You look like you could do with something strong under your belt.' His over-exaggerated wink made Fraser grin self-consciously.

'Bit early for that.' Even if he did feel like something to anesthetise the gnawing hope and worry churning his gut.

'Maybe we should have brunch first,' Allan teased, a cheeky grin so like Nikki's on his face.

'Definitely presents first.' Nikki clapped her hands and began shooing them all up the steps and along the wide veranda to where the huge Christmas tree stood in pride of place.

There were truckloads of presents. Fraser gaped. Never in his life had he seen anything like it. 'Blimey.' This was going to take hours.

Nikki giggled as she slipped her hand into his. 'Told you Mum goes overboard. Anyone who comes up our drive today will receive a little gift, even if they haven't been invited.'

A lump blocked Fraser's throat as his eyes searched the pine tree for the gift he'd placed there yesterday. There, near the top, sharing a tiny branch with an angel, hung the precious object. So small and yet monumental in its significance.

'Are you all right?' Nikki nudged him. 'You've gone all pale.'

If only you knew. 'I'm fine. Who'd have believed four months ago we'd be spending Christmas together?'

Her laughter tinkled on the air. 'Not that I regret any of it.'

Thank goodness. 'Coming home turned out to be the most right thing I could ever have done.'

'Hey, are you two joining us?' Allan called from his Santa seat. 'I'd like to start handing out the presents.'

'Go ahead, Dad. Sorry, Santa.' Nikki tugged Fraser to a cupid chair and pushed him down, then sat on his knee. 'Ready when you are.'

Fraser gulped his champagne and the bubbles shot up his nose, causing him to sneeze. The moment was getting closer. There was no escaping now. Not that he wanted to. But he'd certainly jumped in the deep end. What had happened to doing things quietly and privately? Nikki had happened, that's what. This was about her, for her.

Presents were passed around to everyone and the delighted cries of thanks and excitement momentarily distracted Fraser. The girls especially seemed ecstatic, getting enough presents to keep a small nation going. Even he had never had so many. He unwrapped CDs and DVDs, an All Blacks jersey, a pair of cricket shoes, and from Nikki a voucher for a mystery weekend away for two.

'You're taking me, of course,' she chirped, and for once he saw no uncertainty in those azure eyes studying him from under long lashes.

'Do you know where we're going, or is it a surprise for you too?'

'I know exactly where we're headed. I didn't want to go anywhere not romantic enough.'

'We'd make it romantic no matter where we went.'

'Aw, you say the nicest things.' Her lips brushed his. Her scent filled his nose, tipped his world sideways. He was such a lucky man.

'Okay, you two,' Jay chipped in. 'That's the presents done.' Then he banged his head with the palm of his hand. 'Oops, wrong. Seems like there's one more at the top of the tree.' He looked around at everyone, his cheeky grin finally aimed at Fraser. 'Eh, mate. Your turn, I believe.'

Fraser froze. The moment he'd been anticipating with excitement and a dash of trepidation had arrived. Everyone was watching him, waiting with happy anticipation. Everyone except Nikki.

'What's going on? Fraser, what does Jay mean?' She squirmed around on his thighs, peered at him with a big question in her eyes.

For the life of him he couldn't move. Not because Nik was sitting on him but because his muscles had forgotten how to work. His legs were like custard. His arms gripped the sides of the chair, unable to manoeuvre him upwards.

'Nik, shift your butt and let the man up.' Jay ducked as a wad of scrunched wrapping paper flew at him.

But at least Nikki stood up, turning to stare down at Fraser again. 'Please tell me what's going on.'

The tiniest wobble in her voice propelled Fraser out of the chair and had him reaching for her hands. ‘It’s okay, sweetheart. It’s all good. Trust me.’

She squinted at him, her mouth twitching as though she was trying hard not to smile at him. ‘You’ve hung some of that terrible plastic mistletoe somewhere, haven’t you?’

‘It’s right up here.’ He tugged her with him as he approached the tree and reached up to remove the last present. Then he sucked a huge breath, winced as his injured lung protested, and knelt down in front of her. ‘Nikki Page, please, will you marry me?’

Nikki gasped. The hand he still held began trembling. Her eyes widened in astonishment. She didn’t say a word.

There was utter silence on the veranda. Not even the cattle in the nearest paddock had anything to say. The world was waiting on Nikki.

In his chest his heart was trying to pound its way out through his ribs. *Say something, please.* Yes. No. Anything but this awful silence. He could barely wait.

Nikki blinked. A tear escaped, ran down her

cheek. Her mouth widened slowly into the most beautiful smile he'd ever seen. 'Yes.'

Relief surged through him, lifting him back on his feet. 'Really?' His mouth was split wide in a grin. 'Really?'

'Yes, Fraser, I will marry you.'

The whole room erupted in clapping and cheering.

Nikki leaned in against him, wrapped her arms around him and kissed him long and tenderly.

He kissed her right back, long and tenderly.

Of course, it was Jay who interrupted them. 'Haven't you forgotten something, you two?'

Pulling his mouth from Nikki's, Fraser stared at him. 'What?'

'The small matter of the last present.'

Fraser rolled his eyes. What a dope he was. He took one of Nikki's hands and placed the tiny box in her palm. 'Nikki, sweetheart, you need an engagement ring now.' And he closed her fingers around it.

Her one tear turned into a torrent as she tore the ribbon off and then snapped the lid back. 'Oh, my goodness, it's beautiful. Stunning, fabulous. A bigger version of the first one.' She sniffed.

'You like it, then?' Fraser took the sapphire and diamond ring from its cushion and slipped it over her finger.

Nikki gazed at her hand, holding it out to the sunlight. 'I love it. But nowhere near as much as I love you, Fraser.'

Then they were surrounded by everyone trying to shake hands, hug them, see the ring. The melee finally stopped as Allan and Jay began handing around more glasses of champagne, this time top-shelf champagne.

Allan raised his glass. 'A toast to Nikki and Fraser.'

Nikki hesitated, understanding finally dawning. 'You all knew Fraser was going to propose today. Did he ask you all for my hand in marriage?'

As everyone answered in the affirmative, she turned back to Fraser with a cheeky smile. 'That was very brave of you.'

'You're telling me!'

'I suppose you've all decided when we're getting married too?' Then her gaze turned on her mother, and when Rose's face turned crimson Nikki gasped. 'You have. All those boxes in the spare room. They're to do with our wedding, aren't they? Nothing to do with second-hand shops at all.'

'Not a thing. It was the only explanation I could come up with when I found you about to delve into those cartons of table settings.' Rose gave her daughter an understanding look. 'It is your day, love. There're still lots of things to organise and decisions to make about colours, flowers, the dress.'

Nikki looked around for Molly. 'I think we can sort the dress out right now.'

Molly brushed tears from her face and came to give Nikki a kiss. 'At least we know it fits.'

Fraser looked at the two women he loved most. 'What's going on?'

'You're not the only sneaky one around here. When we were packing up your mum's things while you were lying on your back in hospital, we came across Molly's wedding dress.'

'And you just had to try it on?'

'Of course. It's beautiful.' Nikki frowned. 'When are we getting married?'

'How about New Year's Day? Start the year off as we mean to go on.'

This was where everything could go pear-shaped. Nikki liked to be in charge, and to have partially organised her wedding without her knowledge had been a risk, but there'd been no other way to have the wedding so soon. The licence had been arranged, the caterers booked, the marquee ordered. But Fraser knew they had to get married quickly for Nikki's sake. He couldn't stand for her to fret that he might opt out before the day. Even waiting a week might seem an age for her if she was worrying he might not show up. She loved him, trusted him, but if there was even a smidgeon of doubt about her own worth, that would fester away within her. He wasn't taking the chance.

'We've got a date, Fraser McCall.' Her kiss was sweet and sexy and loving and all the things that made up his woman. 'Second time lucky, eh?'

New Year's Day

The sun shone brightly from a perfect summer sky, glinting off the sides of the huge white marquee erected on the front lawn of Nikki's family home. All the lawns were immaculate, the grass no doubt scared to grow a millimetre since Fraser and Jay had mown and raked them two days ago. The rose beds were stunning with their bright red, yellow, pink and white blooms. In the paddocks to the west of the house the vines were covered in bright green foliage.

A trail of scattered rose petals led from the house to a huge oak tree under which the marriage celebrant stood patiently waiting in front of at least a hundred guests. Among those guests were all the full-time crews from the station and, biggest surprise of all, his friends he'd travelled with, who'd flown out from England two days ago.

Fraser's mum and dad grinned and waved to him as his gaze found them at the front. He hadn't seen them look as happy in years. Thankfully, today was one of his dad's better days and he knew exactly what was going on.

Everything was going perfectly. Even the baby had obliged and arrived between Christmas and today, giving Yvonne time to recover for the wedding.

Fraser crossed to his favourite garden—the

peony bed. The heady scent filled his nostrils, and he snapped off a pink bloom and poked it into his buttonhole. The breath caught in his throat. Never in a million years had he imagined this day quite like this. It was the perfect backdrop for his beautiful bride.

'Where *is* Nikki?' Jay had followed him and now stood beside him, tapping the toe of his shoe on the path. 'You'd think she would be on time today of all days.'

'I'm the one who's supposed to be nervous, not you.' Fraser grinned at this man who was standing up with him at the ceremony. 'She'll be here.'

And there she was, standing at the top of the three steps leading down to the lawn, her hand on her father's arm. Fraser forgot to breath. Beautiful didn't begin to describe Nikki. Dressed in ivory satin that highlighted her blue eyes, she looked perfect. 'Wow.'

'That's my sister?' Jay grinned. 'She does scrub up all right, doesn't she?'

'All right? She's stunning,' Fraser croaked.

'Amber looks awesome too.'

Amber? Oh, yes, tucked in behind Nikki, she looked pretty in her long pink-and-white dress, but his eyes returned to Nikki. He couldn't get enough of her. He heard the guests gasp as they turned to watch Nikki descend the steps and fully agreed with them.

'I've never seen Amber in a dress,' Jay muttered.

Fraser decided he'd be telling Amber to wear one all the time if the star-struck expression on Jay's face meant what he thought. Amber had spent months trying to be noticed by Nik's brother and all she'd had to do was wear a dress. He grinned to himself. What a great day.

Finally, Jay nudged him. 'Come on, man, time you got hitched.'

Then he was being tugged by his future brother-in-law to the front of the excited guests, where he turned to watch the progress of his bride. His heart leapt with joy within his chest and a lump the size of a brick blocked his throat. Everything that had happened over the past five and a half years had been worth it to experience this moment.

When Nikki and her father reached him, Fraser couldn't resist leaning in for one little kiss. 'You're absolutely beautiful, my love,' he whispered around the lump. 'You're everything to me.'

My future, my life, my everything. Thank goodness he'd come back to Blenheim. If there was one thing in his life he could thank his father for it was forcing his hand to come home. Home was where their families were.

'Let's get married.' She smiled that sweet smile that he'd dreamed about every night since he'd first set eyes on her trying to catch tadpoles in the pond behind the farmhouse.

Taking her hand, he smiled back. 'Let's.' And he gave her another wee kiss for luck before turning to the marriage celebrant. 'I think we're ready.'

A few years later

Fraser slowed for the turn into the drive leading up to the farmhouse. 'Are you ready for this?'

Nik shook her head at him. 'This is family, Fraser, nothing more, nothing less.'

He grinned. 'Exactly.' Pressing his foot down

on the accelerator, he added, 'Hope someone's got the beer cold.'

'This is my family.'

True. 'It will be icy cold.' They rounded the bend. 'Oh. My. God.'

'Fraser, Little Miss Big Ears.'

'Sorry. But—' He waved a hand in the direction of the house. 'That's over the top.'

'That's my family.' Nikki chuckled. 'Though they seem to have gone overboard today.'

WELCOME HOME
DR AND MRS MCCALL
AND WEE CINDY

The banner stretched from one end of the house to the other. Underneath crowded all their family, holding glasses of champagne.

'Marry one Page and get a whole book.' Fraser brought the car to a halt and leaned over to pat Nik's expanding belly. 'You might want to stay in there, little man. It's a lot quieter.'

'Daddy, lots of people.' Cindy leaned forward in her child car seat.

'Tell me something I don't know, little one.'

He opened the back door. ‘Come on, sweetheart, time to catch up with all your family.’ He kissed the top of his daughter’s head. ‘You don’t know how lucky we are.’

* * * * *

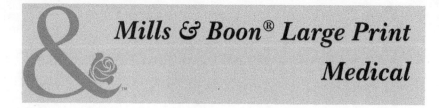

Mills & Boon® Large Print Medical

October

NYC ANGELS: UNMASKING DR SERIOUS	Laura Iding
NYC ANGELS: THE WALLFLOWER'S SECRET	Susan Carlisle
CINDERELLA OF HARLEY STREET	Anne Fraser
YOU, ME AND A FAMILY	Sue MacKay
THEIR MOST FORBIDDEN FLING	Melanie Milburne
THE LAST DOCTOR SHE SHOULD EVER DATE	Louisa George

November

NYC ANGELS: FLIRTING WITH DANGER	Tina Beckett
NYC ANGELS: TEMPTING NURSE SCARLET	Wendy S. Marcus
ONE LIFE CHANGING MOMENT	Lucy Clark
P.S. YOU'RE A DADDY!	Dianne Drake
RETURN OF THE REBEL DOCTOR	Joanna Neil
ONE BABY STEP AT A TIME	Meredith Webber

December

NYC ANGELS: MAKING THE SURGEON SMILE	Lynne Marshall
NYC ANGELS: AN EXPLOSIVE REUNION	Alison Roberts
THE SECRET IN HIS HEART	Caroline Anderson
THE ER'S NEWEST DAD	Janice Lynn
ONE NIGHT SHE WOULD NEVER FORGET	Amy Andrews
WHEN THE CAMERAS STOP ROLLING...	Connie Cox

0613 LP 2P P2 Medical

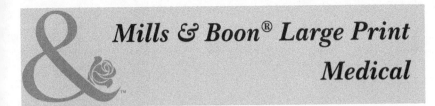